Sir Winston 'Bulldog' Thatcher

KBE DSO QGM

The unauthorised autobiography

Robert E Harris

© MMXX Robert E Harris

This book and its content are copyright of Robert E Harris - © Robert Harris 2021 All rights reserved.

Any redistribution or reproduction of part or all of the contents in any form is prohibited

1. **Introduction,** the action of introducing something
2. **Testimonial**, a formal statement testifying to someone's character
3. **The Early Days.** From birth to schooling, spoiler alert not much happened I was young
4. **Schooling** education received at school
5. **University**, it's like schooling, but for the educated (except media or sociology students obviously)
6. **Military Life**, like university but for gentlemen, (or underclass if you haven't been awarded a commission).
7. **New Arrival** (into the regiment not birth, that would be mental)
8. **Peace Keeping** (squaddies going out and preventing trouble, outrageous but true)
9. **Back in the UK** (apparently Blighty is now referred to as UK, until the Jocks spoil it with their independence lark)

10. **The Troubles** a truly British way of describing the bloody horrors of battle, but on home soil.
11. **Cavalry**, much like being in the infantry but sat down more and less working-class folk
12. **Love**, a word invented by the French and used by Ladies, (*I sincerely apologise for using the term but heaven forbid I upset a feminist*)
13. **Kosovo**, a tad like Bosnia with US/UK flexing their muscle for a President and Prime Minister to gain some sort of sexual arousal.
14. **Grief,** another term invented by the French, the stiff upper lip now out of fashion
15. **Whitehall,** where the powerful and the mighty of this fair nation undertake important business decision and then disguise them as military problems to sell them to tabloid readers.

16. **Iraq,** a stunning nation destroyed for oil oh and of course Weapons of Mass Destruction, can't forget about them.
17. **Afghanistan,** like Iraq, but less oil, more mineral and opiates, but our main purpose was to quash the CIA fund Taliban.
18. **Future,** the part of life in front of us.

Introduction

<u>Sir Guy Cheshire, KBE, AFC, RAF (ret'd)</u>

I have had the pleasure of knowing Bulldog, for what seems like many years. I have without any shadow of a doubt always found him to be an unresolved, hedonistic and decadent example of the elusive British male. He is a loyal, dependable, honourable, gallant and chivalrous, gentleman who knows how to serve a good quality Port. Qualities that this country is tragically and disastrously losing since the fall of the Empire and Brexit. Bulldog, and I reminisced and yarned over the past months together in the Officers Mess many years ago in Northern Ireland a despicable place, but serves a lovely drop of whiskey and the stout is rather magnificent, the NAAFI is run by the Paddy's but I have to admit, the decent ones. I would also strongly recommend the spit roast.

  We met again towards the end of his career and that is when he generously dictated his life story and his memoirs to me over a couple of nights, his words inspiring, thought provoking, galvanising and rousing all at the same time and at once.

  Bulldog, would sit in the Mess and discuss an assortment of subjects from the chances of the light blues rowing team or the calibre of recruits being sent from the counties to regiments in the land. Burning questions that at times led to some impassioned arguments as Bulldog always rated the 'county' boys in favour of less fashionable schools like Westminster, Charterhouse and Rugby. As he always said, the poor end of the elite schools always produced good under officers for the Harrow, Eaton and Saint Paul's boys to order about. Amongst his men Bulldog was esteemed, admired and I venture say at times quite possibly respected. For a gentleman brought up in correct counties of England he had a remarkable ability to speak with the working classes, in a manner that wasn't overtly condescending (he didn't talk down to them). I believe his men adored that about him. He had a skill of speaking with working class chaps from all corners of the nation, even Northerners.

His military career started at The Military Academy after finishing Saint Paul's and of course Saint Thomas Aquinas College; he settled into military life easily and yes, military life settled into him, such is the mark of an upstanding man. After all, his father, uncles and grandfathers were all graduates of The Military Academy and some of the senior officers had family connections with Bulldogs. I believe the former Academy Lieutenant Colonel is married to Bulldogs cousin, rather strange girl, but she plays a mean had at bridge.

This book presents the true Bulldog to the nation, an honest, hardworking chap, who prides himself on traditional values. A man who believes strongly in the what I believe is now disgracefully termed 'the commonwealth'. I dearly hope that you find in his words, a sense of the true gentleman. I have no doubt he will inspire you, and for the sensitive types touch you, in an emotional way. Bulldog spoke openly, candidly and honestly about his life. For that and the Port I am tremendously grateful. I know you will feel a sense of pride and at times emotions as you devour every word of this true British hero. Sir Winston 'Bulldog' Thatcher KBE, DSO, QGM

Testimonials

Sir Peter de Hughes KBE, DSO

Bulldog truly is a leader amongst mere leaders, a man of greatness that inspires greatness, and thrust greatness upon those needing greatness. He gave his all to this nation and to some rather lucky debutants. A British military man that is now out of favour with the gutter press. A man people were proud of before 'key workers' became popular and respected.

Bulldog, is what Britain is all about, good breeding, discipline and the ability to savour a glass of Port, qualities I am afraid are no longer seen as 'popular' in this now devastatingly excuse for a country, I personally blame new Labour, well to be fair I blame all working-class political parties. What ever happened to graduates from the correct universities entering politics, to secure the future of the country, claim expenses and gain directorships in large companies; I could go on.

Major Harold 'Harry' Thompson OBE

I met Bulldog many years ago, watching a rather spiffy game of rugby, his passion for the game was outstanding. The absolute detest he had for the first XV, after their dismal performance goes to show his pride and passion for the game and of course his former college, a true gentleman.

Captain B J Hancock MBE

I served with Bulldog in the 2nd Battalion South Yorkshire and Derbyshire Fusiliers. He was an outstanding leader, he rarely patronised the lower ranks, which is a true reflection of the man. He worked hard and played hard, he was committed to his regiment, his port and his totty.

Company Sergeant Major Hollows

Sir Winston 'Bulldog' Thatcher was my former boss.

The early days, what I can bloody remember of them

I have very few memories of my early years, due to my tender age at the time, and lack of interest in anything except sleep and nannies' ample breast, ha, some things never change. However, I was born, like many of my soldiers on an estate, unlike my soldiers my estate only had the main house and three servants' cottages, stashed away in the wooded area, thank god, some of the working classes live on estates with hundreds of other retched working-class folks. Dickensian if you ask me. But it probably explains the in breeding and desire to enter the criminal fraternity, and sense of pride in receiving unemployment benefits, amongst other unpleasant things.

My father was a colonel in the British Army, working in Whitehall, a military man through and through, six feet two and he stood erect as the day he joined his beloved regiment. A regiment that he gave his best years to, and a regiment that would be proud of him to this day, if it were not culled during government cut backs, in part due to 'the scandal' a minor misunderstanding involving the men, waterboarding and some rather prudish new recruits.

Father was a classic English gentleman, his hair was always immaculately waxed and his moustache combed to perfection, he looked very much like a military Freddie Mercury, however the only aids father had, were a butler and regimental driver. Father walked with a military swagger, parading like a love-struck peacock, hoping to accommodate a lady peacock for after drinks entertainment. His men, respected and feared my father in equal measure equally, the sign of an excellent leader. He spoke with a British accent of days gone by, before text speak, and independent television and what I believe is called gangster rap. Father was a simple ordinary man, granted he inherited a large house, a mere nine million pounds sterling and was awarded a Knight Commander of the Order of the British Empire (KBE). But that didn't stop him rising up the ranks in the military and of course British society.

My uncle, Sir Rupert Thatcher KBE was a Lieutenant Colonel, he served with the Foot Guards and was a proud possessor of a full bushy moustache worthy of a true gentleman, his hair was always immaculate and he always presented himself in a manner very much reserved for the elite in society, a proud man, who once had to punch a local youth because he failed to stand for the national anthem at Twickenham, such was Rupert's loyalty to the crown. If he folded money in his leather wallet, he did so with Her Majesty facing outwards, the sign of respect and dare I say, love for our monarch. He later moved into the General Staff and sadly said goodbye to his beloved regiment, a sad day for him and probably some of his men to, I don't doubt. leaving his regiment was traumatic for Uncle Rupert and something I believe played a part in his sad untimely passing. He never got over leaving the regiment, nor his hepatitis.

My uncle, Sebastian Thatcher CBE was a Major within the cavalry, a charming man, all six feet of him, in stockinged feet. He looked like one would imagine a robust Cavalry Officers would look, smart, presentable and with a moustache that would wobble a lady from ten metres away. He would make me laugh as a boy, doing impressions of working-class people, telling stories of their working-class antics. Uncle Sebastian would explain how the lesser educated in his regiment would speak and their terminology, apparently some of them would call dinner, tea and lunch dinner, oh I laughed at the language barrier and lack of education offered to the working classes. Uncle Sebastian would explain how many of the young private soldiers, didn't use soups spoons when dining, Oh I would spend many a night chuckling.

Uncle Sebastian was a charming man, who bravely stood shoulder to shoulder with his men most of the time, often following them into battle. Uncle Sebastian was kindly awarded the CBE for work within his regiment and a small donation to a local MP. After leaving the military he went into banking before his retirement and embezzlement misunderstanding*

Uncle Sebastian was cleared of any wrong doing, as his cousin and leading counsel stated in court, the fact Uncle Sebastian cannot explain where the three million pounds in his account came from, does not mean he stole it, Uncle Sebastian was simply paid cash for his charity work he did with some under privileged chav children or something like that. Luckily for Uncle Sebastian, Great Uncle Neville Thatcher QC went to law school with the judge and all charges were of course eventually dropped.

I had a third uncle that father forbade me from ever mentioning. Uncle Walter, he shamed and disgraced the family some years earlier by joining the Royal Navy. Don't get me wrong the Navy has its place and there are some good chaps and chapettes in there. They take us real men to wars, and wait around patiently to take us home again, which is bloody decent of them, if you ask me. But for one of my family to stoop to such a vile act, well father rightfully, instantly disowned him. My then step mother Helen didn't like Uncle Walter, I don't think she ever met him, but she would often talk about her disgust for seamen.

My real birth mother Elaine was a well to do, plump lady from Royal Berkshire, the sort of lady that would be described as having a 'bubbly personality'. I never had the pleasure to meet her. She was taken from this realm, when I was of a tender age of one. According to family members she was a rather prudish lady, the sort of lady that would only indulge in the breeding process in order to impregnate herself. By all accounts a stubborn woman, a trait she got from her father, my great, great uncle, once removed Franc von Puchberg. Apparently, father loved mommy dearly, right up until her accident when she was tragically trampled on by fathers' favourite race horse, Heavenly Feet.

He was father's favourite stallion, soft of coat yet muscles solid and pure from years of good breeding. Heavenly Feet was a stunning Thoroughbred, he spent the latter part of his life out to stud. He truly lived the dream. Mother tragically spent the last moments of her life trapped in a muddy field in agony. Such is the cruel nature of life. Around the house there were several oil paintings of Heavenly Feet, one portraying him stamping on mother, it is a wonderful oil painting and the only image of mother in the house; as father always said one doesn't want to be reminded of the past. A remarkable statement for a man whom read History at Oxford.

Father being an up-standing gentleman married Helen a month after mothers' death. Life moves on and grief is for ladies and the French as father often stated...

Helen was a lovely filly, shapely in the right places, she was some thirty years younger than father, a little heavy handed with make-up, and she had a passion for clothes of the tighter fitting, and limited on length variety. She had beautiful naturally bleached blonde hair and a wicked glint in her eye, found on some of the more risqué debutants. She had a dress sense of someone much poorer than she was, but cheek bones a gentleman could spank his pipe on. Despite all these traits, she was very a caring and gentle filly, I often saw her walking around the estate with her arm around a maid or two, gently patting them on their firm supple backsides. I assumed however she could be rather authoritarian on the staff we had around the house. With the exception of Donald our butler, Helen replaced all the staff removing the more worn staff and recruiting young teenage working-class girls. I assume they were cheaper, and they made Helen happy, I liked Helen she was almost like a member of the family, such a sweet girl, however she did use the term moist a little too often for my liking.

Helen would make the younger staff wear wipe clean PVC outfits; I assume to cut down on cleaning bills. A strict mistress she was, I would often walk past her room as a young six-year-old and hear a maid panting, being over worked by Helen. Or spanked as some sort of punishment, often Helen would shout out '*you have been a bad girl,*' as she thrashed the young ladies, granted grammar was not her strong point. Father worked away a lot and I assume she took her frustrations out on those poor girls. Some of them would stay at the house, some of the less attractive ones would stay in the guest quarters, Helen did insist on standards, it was probably what father liked about her.

Donald the butler was a friendly lump, older gentleman, former Regimental Sergeant Major in fathers' regiment. Father gave him a job after he took retirement. He was a lovely man, always laughing and joking with me, letting me run around the house and have fun. He would sit me down in the evening and read me bedtime stories. Unfortunately for me I didn't at the time understand the working-class accent so most of it was just background noise. Occasionally we would go out shooting, and Donald would let me carry the shotgun, whilst Bessie the family Labrador would run around picking up grouse and other animals we culled for environmental and culinary reason.

By the age of six Donald allowed me to shoot pray using the shotgun, as he would say, a man isn't a man until he has killed, wise words. There is wisdom in his working-class charm. For Donald's loyal service to the crown he was awarded an MBE one of the lesser awards bestowed by her majesty, but an award never the less. This set him apart from the other working-class soldiers and to be honest I actually liked the man and enjoyed his company. When I was with Donald running around shouting Grouse, I imagined that's what it must have been like for the working-class children on their repulsive estates, minus the grouse obviously.

When father did come home, he would often sit down with my uncles, in the smoking lounge and talk of the glorious times he had in the Officers Mess and the japes he got up to with the chaps. It was these amusing stories that first sparked my interest in joining the army, listening to how father would make his men polish boots all day, as going into battle with dirty boots was frankly not British at all. Something I completely agree on to this day. If a soldier does not present on the battlefield with well-polished boots, is he truly ready for battle, I think not! Should he be even awarded the title of soldier? For if he does not conform to British standards, he surely is merely a hooligan, with a rifle.

 We were like any other normal family, enjoying the spoils of life and worrying about the important issues of the day, tax increase for the highest earners, inheritance tax, whether to holiday in the West Indies or some other part of the former glorious Empire. Issues that trouble many families up and down the land.

 During my down time as a child I would watch films to cheer myself up or to allow the hours drift by, films about engineering like, Bridge over the

River Kwai. or The Dam Busters. Aviation films 633 Squadron or Reach for the Skies, and to throw the navy a bone I would sit an endure The Sea Shall Not Have Them or In Which we Serve. Films from an era, when Britain deserved the title Great. When a chap could face the evils of war with a smart uniform and a pipe. A time, when one stated they were British people stood up and paid attention.

   I would read interesting and entertaining Memoirs on great men of the nation, Winston S Churchill, Memoirs of the Second World. Monty, The Lonely Leader, 1944-1945: A Biography of Field Marshal Bernard Law Montgomery. Code Name: Lise: The True Story of Odette Sansom, WWII's Most Highly Decorated Spy. The Spirit in the Cage, Third book of War Memoirs by Captain Peter Churchill, DSO. Classics that many a young child would want to read, the sort of books most children read when approaching their fifth birthday, stories that would inspire and make the lower regions of the body tingle.

  They were happy times, I would run around the house, annoy Helen as she spanked a young maid, probably for setting the table incorrectly. Donald would spend the day tending the estate, tidying up after me and general duties no parent would consider doing, it really was a joyful time a time that children up and down the country reminisce.

Schooling

On my seventh birthday I started school, I remember it well for two reason, firstly Helen arrived at Saint Pauls School for Boys and was a smash hit with the staff, making my start a little easier. I remember her walking around the grounds in her jodhpurs and knee-high boots, speaking with the school nurse, an attractive twenty something, with long blonde hair and a backside I dreamt about for many a year. Helen and the school Nurse got on famously, in fact I sometimes saw Nurse at the family home when I was on leave, still working as she always did at school however, she would have a rather skimpier version of her nurse uniform on. Another reason I remember that horrendous first day father rather sternly explaining to me that young men do not show emotion, so when he and Helen departed, I was simply expected to bow gently from the neck (*waiters bow from the waist*), and if needs must, I was permitted a slight grin. I obviously refused to grin, as I didn't want to let father down and showing emotion is the responsibility of the Europeans. Vulgar people, with vulgar traditions.

As the car pulled away, I simply bowed, and then ordered one of the poorer boys to take my belongings to my room, a nice chap, he currently runs a financial bank in the city, bloody good chap, he later in his school life played for the second XV.

Saint Pauls was a standard run of the mill school, a main building built in 1712, which housed the rather sterile classrooms. There was a second building built in 1725 this is where the boys would board. And of course, there was the General House, built in 1678 as a resting station for military men, they would stay there and be looked after by local ladies, whose main working hours were after dark. The General House was where the Headmaster was located and the School Orderly. The Headmaster was a likeable man, strict of course, he would cane a boy for dressing incorrectly, improper use of Latin and underperforming on the Rugby pitch. So, like many a headmaster around the country. Our headmaster Mr Michael Saint Michaels MBE, looked like a typical head teacher, he was tall, almost six feet. He dressed in an ill-fitting suit and a dickie bow tie. At times one could guess his breakfast from the odd stain that would appear on his shirt, but in his defence, lobster is a tricky dish to eat. However, he was a clever man, despite having gained a degree from the University of Cambridge. Mr Saint Michaels was happily married to his third cousin Mary a charming lady, whom looked remarkably like one of the popular music band the Bee Gees, her father was very a high ranking official within the Cabinet Office, so she was from good stock.

  The House Orderly was a tall man, shaven headed, ex guardsman. He was in charge of discipline and uniform within the school. He looked like the sort of man that had been involved in many a fist fight during his time, he was battle scared and deranged; in a charming sort of way. He worked in one of the finest schools within in the country but looked like the sort of man that would work within the Prison Service. Each morning he would stand at the main door, and if you presented, with a jaunty hat, or shoes unpolished, he would issue with a Presenting Order. This would require a student to present their entire issued uniform to him at 18:00 hours. If a student failed a Presenting Order, he would receive the cane and a plus one. A Plus One was an extra duty to undertake, usually cleaning the floors of the main building or cutting the grass around the two-acre site. To date no student has ever passed Mr Williams Presenting Order.

I took to school rather well, I enjoyed the correct subjects, the ones that are necessary and important for life. Latin, History of Art, Etiquette and of course I excelled at Rugby. Rugby Union that is, not to be confused with the working-class northern Rugby League. A vile sport played by vile people, whereas Rugby Union is played by gentleman. It was an honour to represent your House at Rugby, an even greater honour to represent the school. If you were selected to represent the school you were permitted to wear a Dull Cherry waistcoat on a weekend or at a formal school function, thus allowing you to show your superiority to the others.

This award did not extend to the vulgar soccer players, as soccer is or should be simply a game for the working classes.

  I enjoyed the sparkling wit and the interesting mix of people school had to offer. In my house for example there was '*nonsense*' Kelly a gentleman from Surrey his father was a Banker. He was called nonsense as he always said the silliest of things, he once claimed Surrey was a good a county as Royal Berkshire, ha, he was a character, not overly bright but a bloody good fella, in later life her joined the Cabinet Office and excelled on their Graduate Programme, mainly due to the fact his father was a very generous Tory party fund raiser, and close friends with an Under Secretary of State.

  '*growler*' Barker, he was an upstanding gentleman his father was a banker also, well, he was before the rather unnecessary legal case for insider trading. Surely a made-up crime if ever there was one, a gentleman dragged through the courts like some unemployed, knuckle dragging youth, simply for having knowledge of stocks and shares. Luckily Barker's father went to school with both the prosecuting QC and the judge, he is now an independent Financial Advisor to the Treasury. Barker also went into banking, despite his repeated failings in mathematics, he was called Growler as all his women were of the uglier side of the spectrum, his wife, a good friend of mine would scare a child from 10 metres away with her facial hair, but she makes an outstanding Bloody Mary and bless her she understands the rules of Cricket.

 chugger' Peters, a lovely rather slim looking chap, his father was an Investment Banker, Peters went off to the Royal Air Force and qualified as a pilot, not fast jets, he wasn't perverted or lacking in the genital area, he qualified flying and helicopters, like gentlemen and minor Royals. He eventually left the forces having obtained the rank of Wing Commander, Peters now works in banking, and he still enjoys downing a yard of ale every now and again, Chugger was the drinker of the group, he would sneak out in the evening down a couple of pints then come back and vomit on the bed of a poorer student from the Wirral .

'*sawdust*' Bellows, bloody nice chap for a Northerner, after university he saw the light and remained in London, he now works in banking, he was called sawdust because after a night out, our house keeper would place saw dust next to his bed so when Parker came in and vomited the sawdust would soak it all up.

Then there was '*fingers*' Anderson, he came from Australia, his father came over to work in Banking, we called him fingers due to his historical connection to thieves, as an Australian he was obviously related to at least one of them, Anderson moved back to Australia and got into banking, before his untimely death, unfortunately for Anderson he wasn't a good a sky diver as he assumed he was.

'*fortis*' Tutt, lovely chap, six foot three, built like a Roman wall, thick as muck, but by god he was loyal, his father worked in banking, Tutt went on to join an Airborne regiment after the Military Academy. He retired only a few years ago as a Major of the battalion, he now also works in the city, we called him *forits* obviously from the Latin to mean strong, but come on doesn't everyone speak Latin? Finally, 'pinkie' Thompson, nice chap, very flamboyant and aware of the latest trends and fashions, he was popular with the ladies but never really settled with one, the old dog. He went to Saint Thomas Aquinas College then worked for a Regional Television Company; he now works in the West End. Lovely chap and still single, despite being surrounded by totty all day and night, what a character, I never knew where the name pinkie came from? But somehow it suited him.

It was during my time at Saint Pauls that I received the name 'Bulldog' due to my high spirits and no-nonsense approach on the rugby pitch. Together we were a rag tag bunch of innocent children, hellbent on making our way in life despite being extremely rich, well-educated and coming for excellent stock.

I spent many good few years at that school, I was taught to a standard above that of a common run of the mill secondary school. I had a lovely house master, Mr Parkins he joined the school straight from university. He was a former student of Saint Pauls; he represented the upper six at cricket. He would give the chaps careers advice and point us in the right direction, what with him being so worldly. He did have a strict nature but a gentleman whom on occasion would lend the chaps a risqué movie to watch in the evening, nothing crude, after all we were gentlemen.

The chaps made my stay at school a rather charming time, we studied hard, we played even harder, we teased some of the poorer students, to help build their character, I later heard 'shaking' Danvers, whom left a year early to attend counselling and receive medical support suffered a breakdown, apparently some chaps at school really did bully him, which is a shame, because that lazy eyed ginger was an alright chap. He never fully recovered as I last heard he was working as a solicitor; poor chap still suffers stress and as a result of anxiety and being on the poorer side he could not study for the Bar.

Some of the staff at school were rather old school and strict, I would often be on the receiving end of a thrashing if my hat was worn at a tilt, or I flagged behind in Latin class. I today still believe if our youth were to receive a thrashing for not having their tie tied with a Windsor knot, or failing to walk around school on the left, then crime would be a lot lower. As discipline breeds a superior class of person. I for one have to this date never heard of knife crime at the top public

British schools, I truly believe this is down to discipline and learning Latin. Working class youths really don't know how easy they have it. Mr Johnson, the school PE teacher would spank us royally each and every lesson. He believed that children should receive discipline to make them stronger, many years later he retired from education due to, as he put it 'pointless political correctness.' He was old school and he failed to come to terms with not being permitted to administer a flogging to children for failing to give 'enough effort' in PE or viciously verbally abusing a child for failing to adhere to a correct line out in Rugby. He left school and the last I heard of him was a rather brief article about him on the then BBC television programme Crimewatch.

  Who can forget Padre, the school vicar the Right Reverend, erm, my Lord, his name passes me by, however bloody good chap, liked a cigar and a pint, never once did he push us to attend church, to be fair to the man, I never once heard him preach or mention the good Lord, he would often bellow Jesus Christ around the school halls, but that was only if his horse failed to win.

The school worked on the House system , they were, Belcher, Lambton, Maudling and Galbraith, all named after the political establishment, one house named Profumo was removed from the roles after the Profumo scandal, although Profumo was an honourable man, he did liaise with a working class girl and that was not very becoming of a gentleman, especially as she was on the challenging side of the moral spectrum.

The students took pride in the house and the member of Parliament it was named after. I still to this day wear my house tie, broad yellow and crimson with a thin sky-blue line, on occasions permitting, like old boys' day when some of the former students attend and watch a game of rugby, before drinking a Port followed by a nice meal and speaking with the upper six about their career options in banking and investment banking.

I of course joined the St Pauls Cadet Force 4th Battalion the Windsor Regiment a fine Combined Cadet Force designed to give chaps with a wide range of military skills, adventurous pursuits, leadership experience and some of the more robust chaps completed the Duke of Edinburgh's Award. The fit of the uniform, the chance for young chaps to fire rifles and of course the young damsels form the local village found the military attire an aphrodisiac. Many a night I spent camping with the chaps, laying under the stars, smiling as the instructors polished our weapons, these were some of the happiest times I had at school.

My first year was awkward as I was a slight boy, I was confident but my build lagged behind some of the other chaps. I did not discover puberty until I was fifteen years of age. Whilst showing after a strenuous Latin class, the first bloom of my pubic region sprung to life, I rejoiced that manhood had appeared and enjoyed a rather rushed but enjoyable manage et une. With the arrival of my pubic bloom and my now breaking voice I shot up and my frame became sturdier and my testicles hung with pride, wrapped in a glorious mane, like a proud lion. My voice went from sweet and gentle home counties drone to a deeper correct English tone. I was now becoming a man.

I developed a good grasp of education and of course Rugby Union, I studied for my GCSE's, they are simply the qualification of the under educated, and are irrelevant in correct society. The finer schools only acknowledge A levels, as a building block of education. Unfortunately, I did not take my A level studies too serious once father had assured me, I would be accepted at a higher performing university. I did however concentrate in the History of Art, as it is a subject a gentleman should have a true understanding. How can one conduct himself at a high society cocktail party if he doesn't know his Munch from his Monet?

The school Rugby Team consisted of a good bunch of men, we wore our Dull Cherry waistcoats with pride, a strange choice of colour for the first XV as the school colours were Green, Black and Red, however we dominated on the pitch, often beating the lesser schools, Eton, Harrow and of course Rugby. Father would often come down to school to watch the games, and speak with the staff, Helen would come along also. Considering the harsh winters, she very rarely covered much of her body with clothes, I assumed this must have been because she was from Northern stock generations ago as the girls from those regions, ironically never cover their regions. I did enjoy those days, mainly as it were the only times, I got to see father, he wouldn't attend parents evening, as he spoke with the staff at the rugby or on golfing weekends. He was often away when I was on leave. Arriving back to the house just the day after I returned to school, such was fathers' bad luck. Helen would attend parents evening and spend her time talking to Nurse or Miss Fallen the languages teacher. I must admit I found that strange as I never took languages, English is spoken throughout the world so other than Latin a gentleman only needs to understand English. Hey ho it made Helen smile so. Miss Fallen was our only female on the teaching staff, obviously all the secretaries and office staff were ladies.

Pinkie was the head of the school drama club the Light Foots, a group of chaps that would entertain us with plays by Shakespeare, or a more risqué number around Christmas period. Pinkie was always the Dame, parading around on stage for the men. I believe his style of acting is called method as for months he would get into character, wearing women's lingerie and make up. He lived for his drama did that boy.

As school came to an end all of us chaps were awarded with excellent grades for our A levels, two of the boys were awarded two A levels, Tutt was one of the boys, but his A levels reflected his dominance on the Rugby field, surely you can't have the captain of the first XV leaving school without some reward, it was money well spent by our parents. We joined as boys and left as men, we understood etiquette, we knew the finer points of rugby and we all had a healthy acceptance of masturbation.

University

After leaving school with an A level in the History of Art, I was accepted purely on merit, to read History at St Thomas Aquinas College. A fabulous establishment, one of the finest Universities in the world, that has managed to avoid the new crazy world of political correctness. It only takes students on merit, and or breeding, thus avoiding ordinary chaps to attend and distort the Universities glorious traditions. I was gracelessly accepted by Weston House, a fine college that attracts many fine academics from around the Home Counties and the correct parts of the Commonwealth. Some of the lesser Houses accept women, or students from the regions and as far wide as Scotland and the Borders. Some of those Houses were not taken too seriously, but they only had themselves to blame teaching such laughable subjects as Social Science, and Political Sciences, Linguistics, Modern Languages and Computer Science, bloody ridiculous. Universities should only teach, Latin, History, Anthropology and Classics. Subjects that are relevant for life and to show academic proficiency. Instead the left wing has taken over and now these students pick pointless subjects, that lead nowhere and for the ladies, well it will make it difficult to find an ideal gentleman friend.

The University was a self-contained place, a stunning mid-17th century building, surrounded by out buildings that were turned into accommodation blocks, a library and a dining hall. The Cockerel and Beaver Bar was housed in the outer court yard, it once the home of a famous English hangmen, apparently a splendid chap, but not the sort of chap you would invite to dinner. The bar was often busy despite its lack of decent whiskey however, it was a fun place and a location I at times got a little quaffed and tried to goose the barmaid, happy days.

It was during my first few days at Weston that I attended the annual Debutants Gala a traditional event at our college and most English Universities one would assume.

A lovely black-tie evening, some of the finest of foods are served, champagne and of course Ports. After a rousing evening of gentlemen bonding, the ladies are allowed into the hall and the debutants with grace and pride are escorted in, to be admired, vetted and greeted by the gentlemen, accepting them into mainstream society.

Many of the girls are led in by their mothers, whom themselves were once debutants at the very same university. Many of the more mature ladies still had a glint in their eye and a wiggle of a firm pair of surgically enlarged breasts. However, some of the more worn ladies, shall we say, have lovely personalities.

It was during this fine evening that I met Sara, a stunning filly, from the home counties a former student at The Bourne End School for Girls. A fine school where ladies were taught Home Economics, Needle Craft, alongside modern unnecessary subjects for ladies such as English, Maths, History. Sara was reading Art at Thomas Aquinas College, and despite our awkward first meeting we developed a friendship. Sara, bless her, she is still embarrassed to this today, however on our first meeting, she got a little quaffed and initiated our conversation. Bless, she knows she should have done the right thing and waited for the gentleman to approach her, however, drinking and mistakes go together like Caviar and fine Champagne.

Sara stood naked of shoe, some five feet ten inches, she was a size ten in modern sizes for ladies, yes, I know a little chubby for a debutant, but she wore it well bless her, she wasn't shy at being overtly chubby. She had long flowing blonde hair as such any debutant should. Piercing blue eyes, like sapphires sparkling in the moonlight and a smile that could light up a fine Cuban cigar; she was blessed with breasts firm and high, with ample shape to feed a handful of young off spring, when the time should arise, and assuming she can't find a nanny to do that sort of thing.

We chatted that evening about my schooling, my prowess on and off the rugby field and I enjoyed her company, despite the fact that I was going through troubles of an emotional and alcohol induced nature. I ended my evening with Sara by walking her home to her accommodation, like a true gentleman I gently kissed her on the cheek and gave her a quick spank of her firm buttocks, before leaving to her bed down, in a positive glow knowing a gentleman had found her company unoffensive.

The next morning, I sat for breakfast in the Mess Hall along with other gentleman from my college. This was my first shock of my university life. The Mess Hall served breakfast; however, it had gone modern and alongside Fried Burford brown eggs; sweet cured bacon, Cumberland sausage, grilled tomato and field mushroom washed down with Earl Grey. They served something called Vegetarian breakfast, European breakfast and, oh it still pains me, Vegan breakfast, which is basically a salad leaf and membership to the Labour Party. The letter I wrote to the Dean that day was both hates filled and scorning in equal parts measurably. Women were permitted into the Mess Hall which some see as progress, others interpret as the thin edge of the wedge. I also noticed a gentleman eating a croissant for breakfast and he wasn't wearing a tie, the vile type of gentleman that no doubt goes on to be an officer within the Royal Marines, or sex offender, apparently there is a difference. Not the perfect day for a young chap starting university.

  Later that morning I attended my first lecture and was introduced to the head of Department professor Victoria Franklin PhD, whom by a stroke of look knew my father, so my studies would be quite enjoyable. Victoria looked rather prudish in her appearance, but father assured me in her younger day she was quite popular with the gentleman. She always presented with her hair swept back, she wore a plain tweed twin set (I am assured she was rather keen on a pearl necklace, on the correct occasion obviously). She gave lectures in a stern forthright manner however, during tutorials she was more relaxed, friendly and had a wicked sense of humour, for a lady.

It was during my first weeks at Thomas Aquinas that father announced he was to retire from his post within the General Staff and take up a position within the city. Father had now become that vile C word, that's right, the C word no one wants to hear mentioned, Civilian. If there is a more offensive C word in the English language I for one haven't heard it. This was a crushing time for me, but emotions are for the French and ladies under explicit circumstances. Also, father was to receive a handsome redundancy payment, and the salary from his new position ran into six figures.

I was selected to join the Oscamson Club during my early weeks at university, the Oscamson Club is an historic lodge for gentleman who enjoy rugby and drinking fine Ports, formed in 1870 and producing fine gentleman ever since. Yes, granted it has a little bit of a reputation for the hazing of the new boys, but come on, who can tell me that light spanking, and ritual humiliation hurt anyone. When I joined, I was slightly spanked by the Chair, lovely fellow, he now works at the Foreign and Commonwealth Office. Yes, I was gently dipped in in cheap house wine, de-bagged and made to run around the university cricket pitch. It is these sorts of high jinks that make Britain a lovely yet feared country. It was not an elitist club, however, to be even considered for the club you first needed good breeding, followed by a recommendation from a club member. From there your family history is scrutinised to make sure you are from the correct families of the United Kingdom. After that you are invited to the club for an informal interview and a glass of Port. I heard one candidate a few years earlier, well he held the Port glass incorrectly and was immediately de bagged and shunned. He never got over the shame and went on become an accountant at a law firm in the English suburb of Wales

The club was frowned upon by some outsiders and certain media outlets. At times our lunches may appear to the outside world as ostentatious, but who can honestly sit their hand on heart and say they haven't spent £3,500 on lunch before? Yes, granted at times a little rambunctious but sticking a five pound note up your bottom before offering it a beggar is just jesting, something I suspect most people have done, and we usually give them the money after some playful tormenting, and one time I didn't wait around for a thank you or change. But I ask you can a gentleman, wearing traditional evening suit and drinking the finest champagne be all that bad? I will accept that Goosing the turkey at Christmas is not for the faint hearted, but that is how character is made.

I started a liaison with Sara, within days of joining university, she was a lovely young maiden. Always presentable, always the designated driver, and always happy to sit and listen to my exciting stories about nights out with the chaps in the Oscamson Club. Our association grew very quickly. On the third date I wrote her, and noted that I believed the time was right to do her the honour of deflowering her. Something many a lady looks forward to with excitement and at times a little dread, a woman has some pressures on her deflowering, she has to wax her lady region, and get the timing right, as a gentleman does not want to gain a rash from fresh growing virginal hair; it would be like giving oral pleasure to a scrubbing brush. For a gentleman there is not as much pressure, he turns up in formal attire, drinks some nice wine, entertains the lady with witty banter and the odd risqué joke. He then simply whacks out his member and has a stab in the dark. The lady is aroused, satisfied and at last made a woman.

The lady cannot under any circumstances be loose fitting when a gentleman enters, luckily pelvic floor exercises were invented for this very situation. Being deflowered is an important event for a lady, and the gentleman to do such an honour is highly important. If a lady was to be ravaged by someone from the wrong social group her life would be ruined in correct society and her delicate vagina would be sadly underused by gentlemen of correct British standing.

On that special evening for Sara, I arrived on time to her apartment, as a gentleman should. Sara had carefully selected some nice wine and cheese for the occasion, we sat and spoke about my day and the jesting me and the chaps were involved in. Sara informed me she had spoken to my step mother Helen regarding her deflowering and how she was nervous regarding such an important event in a debutant's life. I reassured Sara of her fears and assured her that virginity, like many a condition afflicted to a woman, was in fact curable.

Later that evening after Sara had slipped into the silk attire that Helen had sent her, I removed my outer wear and proceeded to make Sara a real woman. Mere moments later I was completely satisfied with my performance as I arrived, and I am pretty sure Sara was grateful also. I found her lady region to be smooth and without being vulgar I can say her vagina grasped my penis tightly, but not too tight, a delicate balancing act as one doesn't want to make love to a vice, nor does he want to make love to the open air.

That night Sara glowed like a true woman, and became a female adult at last. I finished the wine, thanked her for opening up to me and wished her a good evening, before gently spanking her firm backside and leaving her apartment, Bulldog one vagina nil.

We spent a lot of the first term at university enjoying Sara's female form. She went rather speedily from being a delicate flower to a lover of my resplendent male appendage. I for one was grateful to her parents for insisting she studied woodwind at school, I wrote to her father to thank him for insisting his daughter studied the oboe. Money well spent for the university orchestra and our blossoming relationship.

It made me feel proud to watch her bloom. I imagine it is how one feels when the colt they train becomes a champion horse. Of course, you don't need to waste time talking to a colt after one has trained it.

Sara and I were getting on well, I had taken a shine to her, at the end of term one, I took her home to meet father and Helen, I must admit I was pleasantly surprised how quickly she took to Helen; they spent many an hour together. I would often come back from shooting to find the two girls giggling and blushing with an excited glow that a lady gets when her man returns home. We spent many an evening exploring my physical form and indulging in love making of a rather high standard even if I admit that myself.

When it was time to return to university, I had to unfortunately let Sara go, the chaps in the Oscamson Club, were not overly keen on her, so what is a gentleman to do? I would often see her at the house as she and Helen would have sleep overs, pillow fights and girly evenings such was their friendship, Sara took the news of our departure well, and we remain friends to this day, she later had a brief relationship with a good friend of mine, my Uncle Sebastian. They made a lovely couple, for the two weeks they were together, Uncle Sebastian travelled extensively, when he was in the country, he tended to bag a filly for a few days, then move on. He mainly travelled for tax purposes.

For my studies I was learning a vast amount as I was concentrating on the British Empire as my main body of work, I studied something called the Irish Free State. I probably should have paid attention as one of my earliest postings when I joined the military was going to be Belfast. But at the time it seemed a sad and depressing event so I skirted around it. I later found out all about it from one of my Sergeants, it turns out he was a catholic and knew a great deal about what he called the Irish struggle. As I always pointed out to him, if the Irish had got off their arses and built an Empire like the British did then they might not have had a famine at all. He would raise his fist in jest behind my back, and say things in what I believe is Gaelic, respectful things obviously, me being the senior man.

  The Oscamson Club, were a good group of men who made university a worthwhile time, I never saw the benefit of actual study, surely if every student had their father make a substantial donation to the university then a Bachelor's Degree would automatically be forthcoming, for a new extension to the library then one would receive a Masters Degree as I later found out, money well spent by father. The Oscamson Club, were always joyous, having a sniff of Port and a jolly jape, chatting about the world, the stock market and breasts of lady TV presenters and female sports personalities. Important subjects that all gentlemen should discuss. I would spend many a happy hour or two drinking and chatting with the chaps.

I met another young lady after a few months of singledom and healthy masturbation, this time it was very different to Sara, Claudia was not a debutant, but she was from one of the finer families in the area. Her father had an estate near fathers, only his was bigger and he had double the staff. Gerald, Claudia's father made his money from oil, he went from an average multi-millionaire, to a billionaire thanks to the unpredictable world that is the Middle East. He also sold much needed arms to countries that had to defend their natural interests and oil from enemies around the globe and from enemies of their own state. Claudia although not a debutant, she was pure and hadn't been spoiled by another gentleman, in her own way she was a charming lady, six-foot-tall a rather chunky size 10, but that's why they invented liposuction. She was educated both in the United Kingdom and in a rather nice French finishing school. She was at University studying Philosophy, god only knows why.

Claudia bless her, she was desperate to get a degree and have her independence, but she couldn't explain the Leg Before Wicket rule in cricket. Like many a lady of her generation she had her priorities all wrong. But as I always said if Lady Thatcher, could take on and re-educate the unions, then surely women had a useful place in modern society.

On our first date we went for a lovely meal to Claudia's house, a down to earth meal, more casual than a formal evening. We had Lobster Benedict, Truffled Brittany Poussin followed by Caramelised Apple Tarte Tatin, washed down with a stunning Cheval Blanc 1947 St-Emilion. And of course, 1965 Taylors Single Harvest Port. A splendid evening was had, then Claudia and I went into the sitting room where she showed me her trumpeting skills. I must admit she was a talented musician and I later that evening discovered it also translated into her prowess within the bedroom. Although as a gentleman I cannot discuss this, except to say I was very happy with my performance, I believe Claudia was grateful for the opportunity to pleasure me and for the vitamin S that I provided. She, for a virgin knew how to please a man, valuable skills if a woman wants to find and then keep a husband.

  Claudia was a lovely young lady and many a night I took her down by the river. I would tell her about the chaps in the Oscamson Club, she would listen politely, as a woman does. Occasionally I would allow her to speak regarding her studies and at times let her have a political opinion, Lady Thatcher had taught me to appreciate the ladies view on political life. After all, it was the nineteen eighties and women were demanding a say on matters. I was modernising, and starting to believe women may have a purpose outside of the kitchen and bedroom.
  Claudia was a very modern woman, she studied the best a lady can, she always presented herself in a beautiful, tasteful manner complete with silk stockings, and yet she would happily

fellate me on a whim. If it were not for the rather tragic bicycle accident she was involved in, we would probably still be together, or at the very least be having an extra martial affair.

Claudia was cycling home from a lecture one day on her bicycle, when she was hit by a rather bland motor vehicle, she fell from her cycle and landed heavily on the floor, a direct result she was left with a one-inch scar on her face and needed dental surgery to have a minor crack on one of her back teeth repaired. Obviously, it was a tragedy for our love, I knew there and then when I received the news, I could never marry this lady. How could I present her at the yacht club or in the officer mess, with a scar on her face and a false piece of tooth, a gentleman does not entertain a woman that looks working class. Regardless of her abilities to folate!

Claudia took the news of our relationship ending strangely, however her father fully understood and we remained friends up to his untimely end, during a military takeover in a middle eastern country. Ironically one of his own weapons was responsible for his death.

I discovered years later that he read Claudia my letter explaining our relationship mutually ending to her over Christmas lunch and according to her father Claudia's attitude and unnecessary emotional outburst almost spoilt the entire occasion. Claudia, despite her breeding showed emotion and used a word to describe me, that should only be heard in a Rugby Club on a Saturday evening. So, looking back I had a lucky escape, I could have married a woman that makes a scene. How different my life could have been?

It was around the same time that the Oscamson Club made national media, one of the older chaps had fallen on hard times and made up a story regarding the initiation programme of the club, he claimed it was brutal, unnecessary and elitist. My blood boiled when I read the article. Firstly, there is nothing brutal regarding naked spankings of a new member, there is nothing unnecessary regarding a welcome meal. It is a rugby appreciation club obviously the average meal will be in excess of £5,000. And traditions dictate we don't eat the meal, we simply watch the waiting staff poor it into the bins, it is symbolism! As for elitist that was the most laughable thing regarding the whole piece. One of our members was from Avon, his father was a simple company director based both in the UK and US, how could we be elitist? I was so outraged about this, that it spoiled the end of my first year at University, if it were not for 'milky' Turner letting some of the Oscamson's use his family yacht for the summer the whole year would have been ruined.

The summer was a rousing success 'milky' Turner allowed myself and 'Fluffer' Holmes to sail with him and his staff. Turner was called Milky, due to his overly bright white skin. For some reason only available on ginger haired people, he was the type of chap that would apply factor fifty sun cream before switching on a light. But despite is hair he was a bloody good chap, six foot three and built like a good prop forward. Fluffer Holmes, what a character, he was called fluffer as he was a member of the drama club, but always forgot his lines. Some say it was his lack of acting ability others pointed to the fact his parents were cousins, the true answer was never forthcoming.

The captain was a splendid chap with diplomacy as a built-in provision. There were two maids who looked after the yacht and maintained standards. Then there were 'the girls,' higher end escorts who were there as eye candy and on occasion to offer sustenance and help in the removal of stress. I must admit I didn't take advantage of their service, personally I do not suffer stress and I do not tolerate ladies that feel they have to work.

We sailed around the med for many weeks, relishing the sunshine and the hospitality. We would stop off 'a shore' as the sea dwellers would say, we would go to a restaurant, have a nice meal and abuse the foreign staff for their accents, their lack of basic hygiene and the fact they never had an Empire, we were on holiday and I still believe those foreign types enjoyed our 'banter'. At times I did get a little lonely at sea, mainly in the evenings, but my time at school had taught me many techniques for masturbation and I accommodated myself to many a happy ending.

My second year in University started off well, I bumped into 'pinkie' Thompson, what a delight he was, always surrounded by the premium totty, and yet he was never interested in any of them. Pinkie introduced me to Tamara a fine form of female design, not my sort really, not from the correct class, she had a slight Irish accent and dressed as if she was a street walker. However, once you got past that, she had a sparkling personality and a rather dry wit. Rather unusual for the female form, but a sense of humour never the less. I assumed she dressed 'modern' as she called it because she was an Arts student.

I remember our first evening talking with Pinkie and some of his friends I went back to Tamara's flat, it was a modest attire but artfully decorated. After a glass of wine, we retired to her bedroom and despite no previous experience with woodwind or any musical instrument she expertly relieved me of my 'gentleman's pressure' with expertise and a charming smile, a technique many an Irish Catholic girl have developed. I assume due to the Catholic no abortion rule, many a Catholic girl performs expertly with her mouth as using the vagina would to too much of a gamble and no doubt a sin.

I found Tamara to be a lovely young lady and decided I would be prepared to establish a relationship with her, she introduced me to some rather strange relaxations. For example, one night she took me to something called a gig? This was not an event for the faint hearted. At this gig, I was introduced to the absolute horror of drinking a warm 'house' wine and to add insult to injury it was served in a plastic glass? I would have been better off staying in the house and drinking my own urine. After suffering the horrors, we moved into a room that was full of the great unwashed people, whom for reason unknown to me were dressed like one assumes a homeless lady would dress. I saw one gentleman, apparently according to Tamara he was a New Romantic.

I can tell you having received fellatio from three separate ladies that there was nothing romantic about this person's appearance what so ever. A band appeared on stage and played some sort of rock music and the unwashed and male make-up wearing romantics danced around. It was an horrendous event and the only saving grace was back at the dorm Tamara, had some lovely wine to wash away, the dreadful taste of the vinegar they served at the gig.

I woke the next day disgusted in myself from attending such an event, after Tamara had graced my member with her Catholic skill, and I introduced her to a form of sexual activity that would assure a lady could not get pregnant. I later left her flat and returned victorious to my apartment, and in desperate need for a shower. We stayed together for a couple of weeks, I had a very pleasant time with Tamara and the gentlemen at the Oscaman Club awarded me with my 'brown wings' for a successful landing in the starfish, a true honour. However due to her lack of breeding I decided never to see her again and had to let her go, it was a true shame, but we still remain friends to this day.

I decided to start studying in year two as father was paying a vast amount of money for my education, however, I found it to be tedious and monotonous in equal measure, luckily for me I was able to establish a working relationship with a rather clever young lady, who due to circumstances was not financially stable. I simply transferred monies into her account and she would help me, with writing essays, finding out information and assisting with advice for tutorials. Unfortunately, this did not last long as she was later disgracefully removed from the university for plagiarism. Regrettably for me, this woman was not honest and she used my notes that she supplied me, for her own work. It was shocking to me that people can cheat in such an outrageous manner.

Victoria Franklin PhD the lecturer of my course called me into her office and in a rather embarrassing manner had to speak with me regarding the issue of plagiarism. She informed me that due to my family connections she could not possibly blame me. She was also very complementary on my progress as my work in year two was far superior to that of the work I produced in year one.

The girl in question later went to a provisional university and obtained a first-class honours degree in History. I was truly pleased she sorted her life out and moved forward after the scandal. It is just a shame that the lesser provincial universities are allowed to issue first class honours degrees as it gives the poorer university students ideas of grandeur, that will no doubt lead to them believing that their degree is the same as one from a top five university, it only leads to disappointment.

Year two came and went at University and the end of term was rather uneventful. The summer holidays saw me return home and spend time with father and his new bride. Helen was reduced to the rank of ex-wife by father after she reached the age of thirty-two, after all when a gentleman dines with friends, he doesn't want a timeworn lady sat with him, it creates the wrong impression.

  Helen was allowed to live on the estate, in a rather splendid cottage near the lake. Father allowed her to keep two maids, to help with the up keep of the surrounding area. Father had married a young lady from Thomas Aquinas College, father knew her father and a deal were agreed between the men to allow Jessica to blossom and preserve standards for both families. Jessica was a lovely young specimen, blonde hair, educated to a standard acceptable for a lady, with agreeable hygiene standards. I knew her from Thomas Aquinas College, she was a debutant during my first term.

However, she stayed pure due to good breeding and frigidity in equal measure.

  During the summer my friends Pinkie and Chugger came down to visit and we spent a few days relaxing on the estate. We entertained some young ladies and a couple of gentlemen from the local village. All bloody good chaps, Melanie, was my uncles neighbour. She had known the family since her birth, a striking young filly with an hour glass figure and a flowing head of hair worthy of a Grand National winner. We got on pretty well. She enjoyed a fine wine, and in an evening, she would entertain me. That girl only 20, but already she could ride like a champion jockey. Her ample bosoms, would swing almost rhymical like a metronome on a grand piano, erotic and rhythmical in equal measures. Pinkie forever the gentleman let one of the chaps share his room at night, despite their being enough rooms to go around. But that was Pinkie always thinking about other men.

  The summer however did bring some sad news to the estate. Donald our butler was unfortunately was slayed in a rather strange hunting incident, Father had been out shooting with Uncle Rupert and Uncle Sebastian. They had taken Donald along to carry the weapons and to cull any wildlife that were wounded or dead. The day went well, father had a remarkable hunt and as Donald was loading the last of the weaponry back into the vehicle father reversed as he was in a rush to return home, and as he recanted Donald was taking too much bloody time. Donald was accidently and tragically run over. Father after checking there was no damage to the vehicle, weaponry and deceased animals in the vehicle, summoned for help. However, it was too late for

Donald he was pronounced dead later that day on arrival to a National Health Service Hospital.

To this day I wish Donald had private health care, however, he would rather spend his wages on rent to father, fees for the use of the family car to drive around the estate, and with diesel prices on the rise, he also spent a large amount of his remaining salary on what I believe are called frozen meals, it was a real shame, especially as the ambulance passed a private hospital on route to Donald's final destination.

Donald's funeral was a sad affair, father arranged for some of the private soldiers from the former regiment to carry the coffin. Donald's two ex-wives attended. One of whom wore dark blue not the traditional black to the event. Father was outraged by this and had our new butler Harold remove her from the service.

After the funeral Donald's body was taken to a local cemetery. We of course did not attend this part of the service, mixing with working class people in a council run cemetery sounds rather unpleasant and depressing. Father did contemplate allowing Donald to be buried on the estate, however, despite knowing father for thirty some years, and not wanting Donald to be laid to rest next to civilians, he was not family so tradition would not allow such an act. It was a sombre occasion and one I choose to forget after I accidently vigorously fornicated with one of Donald's ex-wives, a more mature lady, but she took care of the body work. Grieving can make a man do the most peculiar of things.

That summer saw some changes on the estate, a new butler and a new wife for father, change is never easy but Jessica was young and healthy, and Harold was a far better butler, so luckily all was well. I was almost sad to see my friend Melanie leave, the previous night I had considered doing her the honour of a proposal of engagement to later be married. However, as the evening drew to an end myself and Melanie stayed in the garden and she presented me with a going away present by kneeling in front of me and exploring my manly area. It was during this enactment when I had expelled my love that Melanie uncouthly spat out my generous donation. I was raging, what sort of lady would expectorate such a gift and in a public place. I ended the relationship the next morning. I bare no ill will to her, and I was even best man to 'Sawdust' Bellows when he married her the following year. They have a couple of children now. One of them A young chap, let's just say he will probably play the clarinet in the school band if you know what I mean, and a daughter whom wasn't blessed with looks or personality, but she will marry well due to breading.

Year three at university, saw me having to apply for The Military Academy, known throughout the world for its excellent production of military officer and gentlemen alike. The Military Academy was a strange place though. For it allowed anyone to apply subject to qualifications. So, women and working-class people could apply and on occasions they were accepted. Granted they had to attend a strict two-week elocution seminar, and etiquette tutorials. This allowed them to be able to communicate correctly in the Mess. However, I still found the whole thing rather laughable. If the ordinary soldier thought for one minute that his superior was not educated at a fine public school, there would be anarchy amongst the ranks how could a private soldier respect an officer from some drab suburban estate.

I took selecting which regiment I would join very seriously, I had already ruled out the Household Regiments, Although I highly respect them, any division that mixes the North of England, the South of England alongside the Welsh, Scots and Irish, well they can't be taken seriously as soldiers or gentlemen. How would one ever get over the language barrier with some of these chaps. I also found out that a chap at Saint Pauls was joining a Household Regiment and he went to a public school, however he went on a scholarship, so basically a comprehensive kid, however he was good at rugby and played for the second XV.

I ruled out the Cavalry, it has for many years been mechanised and therefore to call oneself a Cavalry

Officer without riding a horse into battle seemed insulting to me. The Welsh and Scottish regiments were out, I admire the Scottish, I adorn a kilt for many a social event, letting my member swing free, as is the style. I drink their whisky, but to this date I have never been able to understand that drone of an accent they are cursed with. I definitely could not join a Welsh Regiment, I have always been affronted by the Welsh claiming to be a country, the place, lovely as it is, is a Principality. Granted the Laws in Wales Acts 1535 and 1542 makes Wales full and equal part of the Kingdom of England, therefore turning the entire place into what is basically a county, consequently the claim to be a county and have national teams in sports is laughable and something I would not take part in, also how could a real country fly a flag with a mythical creature in the centre?

I spent many an hour with the colonel of the Saint Pauls Cadets 4th Battalion the Windsor Regiment (V), Lieutenant Colonel Michael Davis – Holmes CBE. A lovely chap who had served as an instructor with the Regiment for over thirty years. His advice was of course invaluable to me. I visited a couple of regiments to see if they were to up the standard of a privately educated man, and to try a selection of wines and ports in the mess. Together we came up with a short list of regiments that I would consider applying for. It was a difficult time and one, the local chavs at comprehensive don't have to deal with. Those chaps have life so easy.

Pinkie would often tease me telling me if he joined the service it would be Royal Navy for him without a doubt; occasionally he did mention joining the Royal Air Force as their uniform is lush, which I assume is a shade of blue.

Pinkie was a fun chap to hang around with, he knew a surprising large number of younger gentlemen friends, and still does to this day. He once took me to a gentleman's bar he frequented. I can honestly say it was not the sort of gentleman's clubs I was used to, at our club, we do not allow 'pumping' music and a gentleman must always keep his shirts on. However, the chaps he introduced me to were cracking sorts and I must admit I had a very interesting evening.

During my final week at university Victoria Franklin PhD assured me that my degree would be forthcoming and that my fathers' contribution to the History department was gratefully received. Tamara and a friend of hers Debbie, were guests of mine for my final evening. We stayed at her flat and drank a large quantity of wine and spoke about life and the charges facing us in the future. That evening was my first adventure into the world of the Ménage a trois, myself Debbie and Tamara spent a few enjoyable minutes in her bedroom exploring each other's private regions, once I had expressed my enjoyment, I left the two girls to what I believe is called a Ménage a deux., whilst I finished off some wine and enjoyed a firm and strong Cuban. It was an enjoyable end to university life.

Military Life

After leaving university with a second-class degree in History, and a forthcoming Masters once fathers' cheque had cleared. I was selected to the Military Academy, a stunning establishment set in the heart of Hampshire. The main building dating back to the 1600's. Driving up the main gravelled drive you could smell the tradition and the aroma of boot polish flowing in the early evening breeze, a scent I still find erotic to this day. The building rising to its stunning peak as you drove closer. That journey in the car was one of the most erotic experiences of my life.

  I was escorted to the Military Academy by Helen and of course Harold the family butler, father was to meet me there with Jessica as he was attending a formal lunch at the academy with Colonel K P Norris – Eccles CBE, DSO.

Jessica was waiting for me as I arrived, wearing a splendid summer dress complementing her youthful glow, the sunlight behind it, did not leave me in any doubt to her or fathers' preference in under attire. Helen dressed in less formal black skin tight dress and high heeled boots, her hair in pigtails, but the staff at the college obviously accepted her dress code as many a Non-Commissioned Officer (NCO) came over and spoke with Helen and the family, but strangely mainly Helen. Father popped by to wish me well before leaving for an important deer hunt in Scotland. Jessica and Helen left the Academy with Harold, much to the disappointment of the NCO's, Helen had obviously made an impression on the chaps.

In the induction to the Academy we were introduced to the College Warrant Officer. The College Warrant Officer was one of the most senior None-Commissioned men within the Armed Force. He was a strong built man, with a strapping moustache, worthy of a military man. He stood six feet tall, his uniform immaculate and his posture, erect and proud. On his manly chest were medals that were gleaming, including the MBE, proving that this man was worthy of such a posting. He was what one would imagine a Sergeant Major would look like.

He spoke in a rough northern accent, but with authority and volume. His introduction to the Academy was poetic, humorous and yet to some scary.

He informed us of our responsibility as gentlemen and officers, he informed us of our privilege and he was courteous. He made me chuckle when he announced

>*"Gentlemen,*
>
>*you will always address me as Sir and, you will*
>
>*mean it."*

I found that to be a very dry attempt at humour, and bless him for cheering us up on our first day.

I had been unofficially accepted by the 1st Battalion the South Yorkshire and Derbyshire Fusiliers, an exciting regiment with traditions going back many a year. I was also offered a place with the Royal Artillery, but with all that firing of heavy armaments one would spend his entire career bellowing just to be heard. Not the sort of thing for a gentleman to do. These were exciting times, and all I had to do was sit tight and passed the rigorous Academy course:

Term One focuses on basic Etiquette, and decision making.

Term two continues the development of leadership skills.

Term Three Military skills

Term Four Officer Cadet's practice for the demanding training exercises in and around the United Kingdom.

Of course, as a member of an established military family, and graduate of a fine university terms one and two were unnecessary, due to superior breeding and financial security.

The NCO's on our course although working class, were bloody good chaps. They understood military life pretty well and most of them knew their place. The military skills part of the course saw the men 'learn' how to lead their troops to battle. I found the whole thing fascinating, yet unnecessary as leadership in the modern British army did not also mean being at the front. Some of the chaps were rather keen to be face down in the mud, getting filthy and playing soldier.

I for one found it unwarranted. It is far easier to lead troops by giving them a rousing sermon and then standing aside as the Sergeants took your message forward. After all the Sergeants, were the experienced pack horses of the infantry a fine body of men, whom over the years had seen it done it and married an ugly woman as a result. Able bodied men with loyalty in spades, and having only life on a council estate to look forward to after leaving the service they were happy to risk it all. That to me was leadership.

My Sergeant on the course was a lovely young chap from the midlands, couldn't understand a bloody word he said but a good chap never the less. He served proudly with a County Regiment. He joined the military as a typical un educated working class man and somehow made something of himself, his mother and if he knew him, his father would be tremendously proud of him. He would joke every morning with the boys, picking up our smartly ironed uniforms and screaming *"did you iron this with a fucking warm can of coke."* I later found out a can of Coke is a soft beverage solid to obese school children as part of their breakfast, and also consumed by builders and other none trades people. I admired him for his attempt at humour and for trying to make life easier for some of the chaps. 'It's time to kick arse and chew gum, shame I'm all out of gum!' Was also one of his morning quotes a charming man, with a big heart, I of course mean, he was caring, not that he had an ongoing medical condition. He would say the most amazing things '*do fucking press ups, until your elbow snaps you tosser*', or '*fuck, I'm almost impressed*'.

Inspirational words to inspire some of the less established names on the course. I checked and was assured he did not suffer with Tourette syndrome. I remember asking the duty medic, his reply was '*fuck off sir you prick*', not sure if the medic suffered with it though?

On one occasion there was a day when we had to go around the assault course, a ghastly day. It was designed to give us an insight to life as a private soldier. Hideous idea I can assure you, if they wanted us to see life as a private soldier, they should allowed us to speak with a local accent, have sexual interactions with a 'lady' adorning poor thought out tattoos and eating below standard fish from a take-a-away establishment. It would have been more pleasant than running around in mud and climbing over poorly constructed scaffolding. However, I knew military life would require some sacrifices so I obliged our training team and joined in. It was a ghastly course. You ran a few feet, jumped over a small wall, crawled along under some wire, swung on a rope over a pool. The rope was insufficient as everyman fell in the swamp like pool. Then climb some scaffolding and run across it.

I completed the course, but afterwards I wrote a strong letter to the training team staff, reporting my disgust and utter horror at such treatment.

Days spent on the range were fun, I grew up shooting and as such had no problems in this area. I found the whole shoot at a target rather confusing as I am sure the military could afford to import some animals, surely that would be more realistic. I joked with the Corporals that we should use the private soldiers for target practice, they obviously thought my japes were hilarious. I spent many an hour firing at a stationary wooden target, emptying my load all over it. Some of my happiest times.

Of course, many an hour was spent marching, which I fully agree with. If you go to London on any given day there will be many an unemployed person, overseas national, or person from the provinces watching Changing the Guard. Marching makes a man. Our drill instructor a Warrant Officer William Dowe MVO, MBE, from the Household Brigade, he encouraged us hourly on the square, screaming away making sure that the standard of drill was set to the highest possible level. *'Sir, I will fucking break you'* were one of his lovely catchphrases, some of his saying were a little confusing to understand. One day he bellowed at me *"sir you march like a monkey trying to fuck a bucket."* To this day I don't know what he meant.

We spent a lot of time cleaning uniforms, pressing our uniforms and polishing boots, I found this to be a strange and pointless activity. As soon I joined my regiment, I knew I would get a 'bat man' to clean my kit for me. A 'bat man' is a trusted private soldier, someone keen and under educated. A man with military pride, but no real chances of moving on through the ranks. They bring you drinks, polish your kit and do all the tedious jobs unbecoming an officer. Until then I ironed my own clothes and polished my own boots, tedious duties, however, it is what separates the soldier from the civilian.

Towards the end of my training, I was interviewed by some chaps from the 2nd Battalion South Yorkshire and Derbyshire Fusiliers, the chaps arrive and speak to potential officers, get a feel for them and decide if they should join the regiment. I wasn't nervous for my interview Captain 'Minty' Davies-

Carter CBE, was an old family friend. His father played Rugby with father at Oxford. The chat was very straight forward, he enquired regarding father's health and offered congratulations on father securing Jessica. I enquired after his father's health and assured him that the recent newspaper article regarding his father and a street walker and his investment bank losing four point six million pounds was unacceptable gutter tabloid rubbish that no respecting person took seriously. If every educated gentleman was dragged through the press for paying an escort of favours, or losing the banks money no other news would be expressed. I was assured by Minty I would be granted a commission within the regiment.

  Then finally the final day arrived, I passed the training, and I was commissioned as a lieutenant in the second Battalion the South Yorkshire and Derbyshire Fusiliers. Father didn't attend the parade, as he had a prior golfing trip planned. Helen arrived with a maid to escort her and that was fine by me and very popular with the non-commissioned officers. Whom spent many an hour talking to both ladies. Helen arrived wearing a summer dress, that was a shade to tight and with the sun dripping behind her, the onlookers saw how she travelled in a more natural style, the only part of Helen that wasn't visible was her umbilical cord. The maid she brought looked presentable in a nice summer dress and for some reason a collar, fashion was never my subject so I never mentioned it to anyone. She seemed a lovely girl and she was extremely polite, always addressing Helen as Mistress.

The parade was fine, the men were all in their smartest Number One uniform, boots gleaming in the bright sunshine, the College Sergeant Major spoke with us before the parade to congratulate us on our achievements. Then the formalities started, normal stuff we march on, a member of the Household attends and waves, then we march off. Obviously, we had a splendid meal afterwards and some smashing Ports were served.

   Some of the chaps, and one or two of the rougher non-commissioned soldiers went out that night to celebrate our achievement, we ended up at a risqué club, where the ladies would give you a lap dance and a happy ending for a mere forty pounds. It was the perfect way to prepare for my new posting in the north. It was also an easy way to spend five hundred pounds!

New Arrival

I arrived at my new base, a fresh faced chap eager to serve the country, I was met by a Major from number 3 company, he introduced himself, showed me around the camp and advised me on which champs would make excellent 'bat men' Important stuff, a 'bat man.' not only looks after an officer, presses his kit, polishes his boots, he is also privy to sensitive information, like which lady stayed at my quarters the evening before. He has to be a fine soldier, bright, not too bright obviously those chaps need to be in rifle platoons for the big push. It goes without saying I didn't want anyone with too much of an accent, last thing I needed was to have a phrase book on hand at all times.

I took hold of my new regimental beret, a splendid Khaki colour, with the regimental cap badge of a white rose over two crossed rifles and a scroll at the base with the regimental motto Rosa Est, simply translated to The Rose. A straight to the point motto. And of course, the Yellow plume, issued after the unit was based on the Canary Islands during one of the wars. Without sounding brash of uncouth when I wore that beret for the first time, even my gentleman's area stood erect, with such magnificence.

My first day with my company the major took me to the parade square and there stood in front of me was a splendid site. Number One Company the South Yorkshire and Derbyshire Fusiliers. Each man proud in this regimental beret and yellow plume. Waiting for their new leader to grace them. The plume sparkling like a golden phallic symbol erect in the sunlight.

One of the young officers informed me that an officer shaves his beret when it is new, I was assured this was not to make it look bigger; it was in fact to make it look neat and tidy. Something an officer should always be. Information like this, is in valuable to a gentleman and a soldier. That is why I eyed my new company for a potential bat man.

  The major introduced me to the men, with the simple words of "Gentleman this is Lieutenant Thatcher the newest gentleman in this long line of leaders, that have proudly served this regiment." You could tell the men were proud, despite their complete lack of movement, such is discipline. I stood silently for a few moments to soak up the atmosphere and to allow the men to view me in my splendour. Before greeting them and informing them of the pride I had in the regiment and of course myself. It was a very brief chat, as then men had duties to perform and I had to go and view the officers mess.

The men were dismissed to their duties and I was introduced to the Company Sergeant Major a rough old northerner. Still had the accent after twenty-one years in Her Majesties Armed Forces. Company Sergeant Major (CSM) Ian Hollows was a formidable man, served in Northern Ireland, being Mentioned in Dispatches for bravery, played for the first XV and was pleasantly married to wife number three Mrs (CSM) Hollows, a girl from a council estate in Barnsley, yet she had no tattoos? CSM Hollows was tall, stocky and rough, all the qualities needed for a company sergeant major and husband, if your wife is from Barnsley.

We got on immediately, I introduced myself, explained how I saw the company working, he explained how he saw it working and we eventually agreed that I was right. The next morning the men were taken off the live firing exercise to concentrate on polishing boots. I wanted them to have the finest boots in the regiment and I was going to have that.

Some of the men, the war types, were not happy sitting polishing boots, for some reason previously they had been on exercise, on the rifle range surely tasks they should have learned in training. If they had learned them, then why practise? Even the working-class soldier can remember to run towards the enemy, and to shoot.

The first couple of months flew by, I was learning new skills, meeting the men and getting to know them. We had our first exercise as a company one weekend. I pitched a tent and lead the men from there as I sincerely believe a leader leads and a worker works. The men spent their day tracking down enemy positions and generally trawling through muddy fields. Then at night I would hold a briefing and give them pointers on any mistakes I felt were made. It wasn't really to my liking living in a tent, however, that's how wars are won in the modern day. On the final day we had a march back to camp. Myself and one of the platoon sergeants had a little disagreement about the route back to camp. I forcefully pointed out that I was the educated man and therefore my route was correct. He accepted this and off we went. Unfortunately for the Company a slight misreading of the map must have taken place and what should have been a three-mile march turned into a twenty-mile march. On a positive note the men got some much-needed fitness training that day.

As we arrived back at camp, late, cold and wet I took the Sergeant to one side and pointed out that an error was made, and his attitude did not help the situation. He spoke to me in an unprofessional manner and had the audacity to suggest I made the mistake and I was unsuccessful with a map. My blood was boiling and I had no choice but to charge him with insubordination. I could not believe a man from an inner-city council estate, with fifteen years military experience could stoop so low. The next morning, I spoke with other officers and it was decided the Sergeant in question would be removed from my Company and be reduced in rank to Corporal. This to me seemed like a satisfactory result.

Later that day and news spread throughout the company regarding the sergeant. The men were rightly upset, they obvious understood he was not a good leader and had to be removed. There mood would last for several weeks, such was there dislike for the sergeant.

CSM Hollows, took drill most days, as the men needed the practice, all good soldiers should be able to march to the highest of standards.

Drill is used for many purposes within the military, firstly its teachers the men to respond to an order immediately and without question. Secondly it enables a large body of men to move from point A to point B in a smart manner. Thirdly the tourist loves it, watching a British soldier march gives our friends from overseas a warm welcoming feeling. And Finally drill looks good from my office window, watching the men parade, makes me feel good so that's why they needed to practice.

Peace Keeping

News broke that due to civil unrest in the Balkans the 2nd Battalion South Yorkshire and Derbyshire Fusiliers were to be sent out there to assist the United Nations in peace keeping duties. On hearing the news, I assembled the men and broke the news to them that the Battalion was to support United Nations Protection Force (UNPROFOR) in Bosnia. I then instructed the Company Sergeant Major to ensure the men spent the week leading up to the deployment ironing uniform and polishing boots. We did not want to arrive on UN duties looking unprofessional. For we were representing the Crown, soldiers from lesser countries would be there and they looked to the British Tommy for guidance, inspiration and heroic prowess.

The British named the offensive Operation Grapple, a beautiful sounding name, one to inspire soldiers. Unlike our American counterparts the British did not simply name operations after what it was, Operation Iraqi Freedom or Operation Desert Storm stupid names, and showing a distinct lack of thought. No, the British used code names to throw johnny foreigner off the scent, and to show we had class. Otherwise we'd be no different to our cousins from across the pond*.

I don't suppose the Iraq war would have played out so well if we called it Operation Seize the Oil

The evening before deployment I gathered the men and gave them a rousing speech to inspire them and reassure them in equal measure. Something a leader does not want to do, however on occasions has to.

"Men, tomorrow morning we will leave our families behind, some of you will say

goodbye to loved ones for the last time. Some of you luckier chaps that don't have wives or girlfriends have an easier time as you are not cared for or loved, making departing easier. Either way, we will march forward and perform our duties as Fusiliers, as Yorkshire men and men form Derbyshire. We will treat our enemy with true British military grit and treat the innocent civilians like wise. We will not show favouritism nor will we discriminate against these foreign types. Our goal is to keep the peace, and keep the peace we shall. May God have mercy on anyone that tries to stop us keeping the peace. Some of us may not return, and lay waste in a foreign field, rest assured your loved ones, should you have them, will be looked after, up until six months when they will have to vacate married quarters. If you die you will be remembered on the regimental wall of honour and your name will live on in the sergeant's mess for many years to come. Even if the sergeants don't know who the name belongs to, they will know you gave everything for the regiment.

Times may be difficult and at times we may feel hardship, you will suffer silently and proudly, like fellow soldiers before us. So, tonight make tender sweet love to your wives, girlfriends or some one-night stand for what may be the last time

God speed gentlemen and God Save the Queen"

I believe the enormity and sadness was felt by the men, as their muted applause could almost be heard as I walked away, towards the officer's mess in time for dinner. Allowing the words, I had passionately spoken sink in for the men. I later had the words printed and framed, I donated it to the Junior Ranks Mess where it sits on the wall to this day.

We posed for a Company photograph all the men wearing the Blue Beret of the United Nations, to be fair, it was a nice beret, but without the yellow plume I felt naked and I didn't like being naked, not in front of the men.

The next morning, we left for Royal Air Force Station Brize Norton and a short journey to our new temporary home in Bosnia. I discovered the Royal Air Force do not do business class on their flights, something I am still bitter about today. The place was a real mess, many towns and villages had been destroyed by war, such a shame as only years earlier I had visited the region on a summer break with the chaps and had a marvellous time.

The battalion was to be stationed in Gornji Vakuf, a nice enough place if one enjoyed civil war and unrest. We were there to do a job, and no matter how tough it got my men would do that job.

The men settled in to life as a peace keeper, vehicles coming and going at all hours, chaps working long hours, at times with patrolling and polishing boots they were awake 16 hours a day. I was thankful I was an officer because if I don't get my ten hours sleep, I am quite the grumpy chap. Luckily due to breading, a good education and financial security I did not have to sleep ten to a room, like the private soldiers. I had a more suitable accommodation.

After a week I decided to join a patrol as they went about their duties. We fired up the vehicles and headed out. The place was destroyed, families living in burnt out shells, scruffy children playing in the fields, dodging landmines whilst attempting to play football. Dead and wounded had previously lined the blood-stained roads. The stench of death filling the sky. One woman we passed was quite the looker, for a foreign type, but her hair was in disarray, she had no makeup on and looked like she hadn't showered for a while. Shame how a lady can let herself go like that. I suspect she would find it difficult to land a husband looking so dishevelled.

We came across some men who looked very dubious, the Company Sergeant Major wanted to stop them, but I assumed it would be a waste of time, but the CSM persuaded me that the men need to be stopped and I granted him permission. The CSM jumped from the vehicle and with a couple of the men approached the youths. They were searched and we discovered they had weapons on them. The men were arrested and immediately taken back to camp. I personally found it pointless but the CSM was an old war dog and lived for that sort of interaction. I firmly believe once in a while you have to let the dog off the lead to have a run around.

At the camp whilst I went for afternoon tea, the Company Sergeant Major handed the men over to the Royal Military Police. The following morning the Police contacted me and informed me that the men in question were actually high-ranking officials within the Serbian army, one of the men had been wanted by the police for several months. As a direct result of this I was to be Mentioned in Dispatches for my actions the day earlier. The men would later learn of this and no doubt, there pride in their superior would be at breaking point. A well-deserved award for inspiring leadership. For the Company Sergeant Major would not have made the arrest if I had not approved his plan. No doubt that is how the Company Sergeant Major saw the award also.

  Sadly, a day later one of our men, think his name was Private Wilkinson or Williamson was tragically killed. Shocking news to be given during a Cornish crab salad, brown crab mayonnaise, toasted muffin lunch. However, being a soldier was not always going to be a pleasant experience. I knew once I had finished my meal and washed it down with a fine wine, I would have to break the news to the men, the men were rightly saddened by this news and needed some time to accept what had happened. I generously gave them an hour away from cleaning their uniforms to come to terms with the loss, then unfortunately, back to work, this is military life, it isn't easy or pleasant for anyone.

A week later, myself, six soldiers and the body of Private what was his name? anyway we were flown back to England, it was a sad occasion. At RAF Brize Norton, I met with his family, his dear, sweet mother, she spoke with me for ten - twenty minutes, telling me about her son and how sadden she was. I caught the odd word here and there; she was upset and northern, her words confused me. Her son was taken to a local undertaker in the north whilst I stayed at Brize Norton that evening, as I had heard the chefs there did an award-winning breakfast. Carrot, Orange, Celery, Red Pepper, Ginger and Turmeric fruit juice followed by Poached Eggs on Toasted English Muffins with Hollandaise Sauce and Rashers of Crisp Bacon, surely one would agree a great start to any day of the week. Well worth the flight over.

  A couple of days after arriving back we went to Chesterfield, a bleak Northern place, famous because some builders put the roof of the church on wrong. The locals took it as a sense of pride and never fixed it, but instead made it a tourist attraction. How the north operates is beyond me; and how a dysfunctional church spire is an attraction is mind boggling at best, if you consider that our Lord Jesus Christ was from a family of carpenters, you would think that poor woodwork on a church would possibly blasphemous.

It was the funeral of Private Williamson or Wilkson, actually come to think of it might be Private Adams. No private Adams different story, bloody good chap, before the accident. So anyway, this poor private what was his name, bloody hell, Walters, Private Walters, anyway he was to be laid to rest in Chesterfield, when I say laid to rest it was a crematorium, so scattered to rest is a more suitable term to use.

The building was bursting with people. Family, friends, men from the regiment and a sprinkling of journalist. The men from the regiment stood out for their uniform were second to none their boots glistening, the yellow plume standing like a beacon of hope in dark times. Some of the local youths, my good Lord, some didn't have suits on, some didn't wear black and one chap, had a bloody ear ring in. Luckily the service passed quickly, and we had to endure the hell that was meeting in a local public house, for drinks and a buffet, I say buffet, but some cold sausage rolls and stale cheese sandwiches would not constitute a buffet where I was raised. I don't think anyone could understand the torture and pain I was going through. I had a glass of what the locals called wine, I made sure one of the corporals stayed with me as he could translate what the locals were saying. The corporal came in handy as the accents were shocking, it is like we left the letter H at the Watford Gap. It was a hellish day for me, but I was strong and somehow I got through it.

  I didn't go back to Bosnia as I believed I was better suited to life in UK, and as I had served over twenty-eight days, I had been awarded my medal, so no real point returning. In the modern age military leaders can lead form anywhere. That was my first experience of being in a war zone and I survived and so had my men. I saw the rest of the posting out, via email, speaking with junior officers and the Regimental Sergeant Major. He assured me he was more than happy with me leading from the rear.

It was during this time, I sunk to my lowest in life, I went out for drinks with a couple of chaps from another regiment, nice chaps but not officers. We went on what I later learned was called a pub crawl. It was during this evening I did something I am terribly ashamed of. I had a one-night stand, not something a gentleman usually does but something a soldier does on a weekly basis. I met a common woman, you know the type, short skirt, bad hair dye, roots showing, and extended finger nails, by a friend no doubt named Tracey. We mated in her compact car I performed a JFK, by this I mean I shot fluid over her face as she wriggled around in the back of the vehicle. I am of course not ashamed of the JFK, something I have performed on numerous occasions rather the fact the act of love was carried out on the outskirts of a council estate.

Back in the UK

Within weeks of the Battalion arriving back to the United Kingdom, I was called in to see the Colonel of the Regiment. A lovely chap Col Richard, Edward Hope-Smith KBE, father went golfing with him during the summer months. Anyway, Dickie called me into the office, and greeted me with a good firm British handshake, smiling, "Bulldog" he said with a beaming smile stretched across his war-torn face. "Bulldog, congratulations you devil dog." I must have had a slight look of confusion across my face. Dickie smiled sat me down, got his orderly to pour some drinks, then proceeded to inform me that due to the arrest of the Serbian and the importance of it, he'd spoken with 'Giggles' Brown from the Civil Service and a former captain of the Thomas Aquinas College first XV, as a result of events in Bosnia I was to be awarded with the Distinguished Service Order. An honour for sure, and one I knew my men would be extremely proud of. Myself and Dickie sat for a while chatting about the award, and other important issues such as the correct batting order for St Thomas Aquinas College when they faced off against Cambridge. I had a splendid afternoon, I left Dickie's office and telephoned the Company Sergeant Major to share my good news with him, it is fair to say he was speechless when he heard the news. No doubt proud of his superior.

After news broke about my award I was swiftly promoted to Captain and I moved from One Platoon, Number One Company to overall control of the entire Company. A great honour, not just for the men, but for me also,

Running the entire company was a challenge, luckily for me I had the company sergeant major on side, there was a little dissent from some of the more jealous officers whom for whatever reason assumed they would be promoted ahead of me. One chap was in line for promotion but over looked. I pointed out to him some home truths during a few drinkies in the mess. Firstly, he hadn't been awarded the Distinguished Service Order. He went to Rugby as a younger chap and then onto Durham University. I mean do not get me wrong Durham is an excellent University, with a good Rugby team and some fine fillies. Yet if you cannot be accepted to a top university, you can't complain when someone who does is promoted before you. He resigned his commission the next day and moved back to London and went into banking. Bloody good chap, if a little hot headed and emotional.

Running the company wasn't a difficult task once I had got the right men in place, the Company Sergeant Major would oversee discipline and drill. If a man can't march, a man can't go head first into battle. I had a couple of Colour Sergeants to do admin tasks and a few junior officers to oversee everything. Once a week I would hold a company meeting and the chaps would report to me, keep me abreast of events. Or if I was busy pop it in an email and give me a general outline.

I also got my first bat man around this time. Lovely young chap Private Jenkins, or Jenson, anyway names not important. A lovely lad, polite, friendly, could polish boots to a high standard and academically he was described as dim. He left a comprehensive school in Rotherham aged sixteen with no GCSE's to mention. Joined up and after training came to the Regiment. I first met him in Bosnia and I remember thinking then he was excellent cannon fodder. Sort of chap you could send into battle, and if he failed to return you wouldn't miss him too much.

  A bat man is an important role, one must make sure that the officers uniform is in correct order, you must ensure he is given a decent cup of tea every morning, you must make sure that the cup of tea served at a weekend is an 'Irish' coffee, but not too 'Irish' a gentleman doesn't want to start the day too tipsy. A good bat man will also make a believable excuse for you when a lady rings and you are already engaged in a meeting or ménage a trois. A good batman will also be able to discreetly escort a lady visitor off of camp in a morning without creating a scene. Also, if the woman is below the normal acceptable range of beauty then he must pretend he serviced the lady, in order to save the officers reputation.

One of the first duties my bat man had to undertake was a sensitive duty. One morning I had entertained a damsel named Denice a lady from the local area, a nice enough girl, however, I called her Butter Face; a cute nickname for a lady, I am sure you will agree, I gave her that name for when one spoke about Denice the first thing one would say would be, '*she has a striking body, but her face.*' She was blessed with a body of angels, curves in the correct place and a piece of rump one would want served on a silver platter with a hollandaise sauce. However, in the face department she was lagging behind many a woman. A Monet I believe the term is, she looks amazing from a distance, but hazy and rough up close. She wore a fair amount of make-up as she needed to cover a few cracks and creases. Anyway, I had entertained her one evening, a splendid performance from myself as one would expect and then the next morning around 06.00 hours, Jenkins came to the room, and saw my predicament. Gracefully he waited for butter face to dress then escorted her out of camp via the married quarters, to avoid men seeing her, he politely informed her that I would be in touch as and when I was not on important duties. I entertained butter face on several occasions, mainly out of boredom and mainly due to her lifelong love of gymnastics her outstanding collection of lingerie and her ability to breathe through her ears if you get my meaning. If she had been from a better background and did not resemble a Picasso, I could have easily seen myself courting that lady on a more permanent basis.

The Troubles

Life was going rather well at the Battalion; I was enjoying regular sexual pleasantries with butter face and my bat man seemed like a decent chap, performing his duties and not becoming over familiar with me. Then one day news came in the Regiment was off to Belfast. A rather interesting place, stunning whisky, a beautiful drop of the black stuff, decent countryside, on a negative side the bog trotters didn't like the British for some reason. Beyond me! Turns out they don't know what they want. Oh, the prodders, well they hated the Catholics and wanted to kill them in order to stay British, simple fools, they were never British, hence the United Kingdom of Great Britain and Northern Ireland, so they were kicking off for false reasons. Now the Catholics or left footers, strange lot hated the British, loved our social security though, well we went over there to stop them being killed by protestants and they for some reason they didn't like that, so they turned on us. The British soldier stuck in the middle of this mess, for no reason what so ever. That was my take on the whole bloody Northern Ireland problem. Anyway, the Regiment was to go over there and support the Royal Ulster Constabulary (RUC), good bunch of men, like a real police force but with rifles and shocking accents.

  I called in my team, and instructed them to stop all training an spend our final week in camp polishing boots and getting our uniforms up to standard, we would show the Paddies how a real regiment dress.

  The evening before we went over, I got the entire company grouped together and gave them one of what was becoming my legendary speeches.

'Gentlemen, tomorrow we head once again for foreign shores, whilst we are there, we will treat the Paddies from all religions equally and with respect. We will not belittle them or cause them unnecessary harm. They may not know how to live in a civilised society however, most of them are still people and as such, they will be treated accordingly. I know in this Regiment we have Protestants, Catholics and according to Private Hussain's records we have Muslims. I personally don't care who or what you believe in, we are one regiment and one regiment we will be. If for some reason some of you fail to return from this posting, I am sure you will be missed, by your families and if you have them your friends. Try not to let this happen, for the last one that struck out in Bosnia brought the moral of the regiment to an all-time low for a few days and we don't want low moral whilst carrying out our duties. Try and stay safe gentleman and remember we are doing this for our Government, our *county but most importantly Her Majesty the Queen.'*

An important and moving speech but I honestly feel it is the duty of a leader, to lead and to do these difficult challenges. I returned to my accommodation, for my evening meal, whilst my bat man sorted my uniform and equipment ready for the trip. Again, I had a copy of the speech printed and framed for the men to keep.

I had a bloody goods night sleep the evening before or trip to Ireland, I had a lovely full English breakfast before travelling to my new home in Belfast. Palace Barracks was to be my new residence for the next six months, run of the mill camp, very busy, Men coming and going all hours. I did mention to the colonel of the regiment how inconvenient it was to have vehicles and men trapesing in and out of camp all night long but it turns out he had mentioned it to the Ministry of Defence and they were adamant this had to continue for operational reasons. Bloody civil servants interfering with military matters, again.

My first day there I was shown around Belfast by an officer from the Grenadier Guards, he couldn't apologise enough for the state of the place, but as I pointed out, he wasn't responsible for city, that was down to the locals. The tour lasted about an hour we drove around some dirty places he pointed out some things of interest and then back in time for elevenses. It was fun though walking around rifle in hand, admiring the Irish ladies and their Celtic flowing hair. The Catholics would play hard to get, giving dirty looks out and being rather rude at times, why, well no one knows, but underneath, you could sniff the Catholic guilt waiting to be set free.

It would be the first and one of the last times I went out on patrol, horrible place, not a single gentleman's tailors in sight. I can see why they throw petrol bombs. I left the patrolling to the men, the working classes love doing that sort of thing. I preferred to sit in the mess or if I had to, I would attend meetings. On a positive though another medal came my way and rightly deserved the hardships I had to endure.

I did have to nip out on the odd occasion, I remember one evening, bloody local youths were having a bit of a riot in West Belfast, something to do with marching by the other side. My men were there having bricks, bottles and petrol bombs thrown at them. A chap called lieutenant Watkins was dealing with it and doing a splendid job. The working-class boys of the regiment were holding the line and I assume many were home sick, being reminded of inner-city life. After five or ten minutes I wished Lieutenant Watkins God Speed and went back to the barracks. Once back at the barracks with a gin and tonic on my desk I wrote a letter to the then Home Secretary suggesting that the Government should look at raising petrol prices in Northern Ireland to prevent the locals from making petrol bombs. It was gone eleven o'clock pm before I finished work that day, and there are people out there that think being an officer is an easy job.

The next morning when the men were back after a night of hard work, I got them to parade and congratulated them on their hard work and British resolve. I also spoke with the Company Sergeant Major regarding the uniforms of the men, standards were slipping some of the men were rather scruffy to say the least. I had them quickly change and wash their uniforms before allowing them to go to breakfast.

That morning I was requested to attend a meeting with the Colonel of the regiment. Dickie was in a chipper mood, rather excitable whilst eating his Scrambled eggs 'en brioche' with caviar. I sat with him and indulged in a Severn & Wye smoked salmon & avocado, toasted rye. During the meal Dickie told me how pleased he was with the Regiments response to the previous evenings folly, and as a result of attending and showing great leadership I was Mentioned in Dispatches,

A great honour for myself and of course all the men involved. He also passed on a message from father, as they had met only the week before at a golf tournament to raise money for a new oil painting at the Regimental Headquarters.

I got one of the duty drivers to take me out around Belfast one day, to give the men a moral boost, we went along and I occasionally stopped and said hello to the odd soldier. However, it started to rain, so I had to pull the plug on the moral boosting and head back to camp. I'm sure the men understood, and after their twelve hours shift, I would have been there to greet them but it was eleven o'clock at night and I was a little quaffed in the mess, plus it was still raining.

The following day I had to fly out of Belfast and attend a ceremony to receive my Distinguished Service Order. It felt comfortable leaving the men behind, their boots were polished so I knew they would survive the uncomfortable pounding of the harsh Belfast Streets. I arrived in London, early the next day I paraded in my Number One Uniform complete with my Bosnia medal and General Service Medal Northern Ireland proudly displaying the oak leaf device to symbolise my Mentioned in Dispatches. It was a pleasant day, I attend alongside Helen who was there on father's behalf, he had a fishing trip planned for that day. Helen wore a rather splendid plain black dress, a tad tight for the occasion and a tad short for any occasion. However, she made the effort so no harm done. I was the guest of honour at Buckingham Palace, HM Queen Elizabeth presented me with my medal and said a few words, I was extremely honoured to be there, the only disappointment was that minor celebrities were there to receive their MBEs for attending Glastonbury or some other nonsense they give these awards for.

After the event I was taken for lunch with Helen by the then Chief of Defence staff. I had a lovely Linguine with aged parmesan winter truffle. The Chief of Defence Staff ordered a rather succulent Veal schnitzel with fried duck egg charred artichokes and rocket Helen ordered steak tartare with egg yolk horseradish, rye toast and French fries. To be honest we had an enjoyable afternoon and The Chief unofficially informed me that due to excellent reports from the Regiment and of course my dear Uncle Sebastian being a close friend that I was pencilled in for a desk job at the Ministry of Defence. However, in order to attend I would have to move from the Regiment to another Regiment to gain experience and such like, bloody typical government red tape. I knew my men would not be happy to see me go but they would understand that people from high levels of society have ambition, as ambition for them is simply a word in the dictionary. After the meal, I was driven back to Brize

Norton to go back to the Regiment, Helen was collected by Sara, the lady whom was my first adventure into relations and former debutant from St Thomas Aquinas College. To be fair she had let herself go a little but she was extremely keen to see Helen. Some may say over familiar, but Sara was one of those passionate types.

  Back at the regiment I assembled my team and sat them down, once Private Jenkins or anyway, names aren't important. Once my man had gone and served tea and light selection of sandwiches, I explained that I would be leaving the regiment in order to move onwards career wise. The Company Sergeant Major bless him, in order to hide his true feeling, he smiled, a broad smile, brave man, no doubt fighting back the pain he was feeling. To be fair to the men they took the news pretty well. Keen for me to move upwards up the chain, they were adamant I left with immediate effect, each one of them to a man, putting my career before the Regiment, now that I say is loyalty to their boss.

I made the move to another regiment two weeks before the South Yorkshire and Derbyshire Fusiliers returned to the United Kingdom. It was a shame I couldn't stay there and see the tour out but my career was moving forward and Palace Barracks was to be honest a bit of a dump.

Cavalry

I decided to have a change from the infantry and move to a mechanised regiment, easier on the feet. I know I did not agree with a man calling it the cavalry due to the lack of horses, but I was modernising. I decided to join the 74th (Edward the VIII Own) Dragoons, a charming regiment using Scimitar armoured fighting vehicles. the Dragoons recruited solely from South Yorkshire, Rutland and The Wirral making it an interesting unit. Their headdress was a khaki beret, the regimental cap badge was a laurel wreath with the letters VIII in the centre and Edward VIII Crown on top over a red square backing. The Regimental motto was Loyalty to the Country, something the late Edward VIII would be proud of, no doubt.

The regiment was based in an out of the way place called Bulford a military

Garrison in Wiltshire a rather interesting place, not far from Tidworth, but luckily easy to get to London and at last some fine restaurants and decent wine lodges, so things were on the up. First problem I noticed on arrival again was the language barrier, the boys from South Yorkshire well they couldn't pronounce the letter H but I had strangely gotten used to that. The men from Rutland, my Lord only knows what sort of language they spoke, they sounded like a farmer had bred with a working woman from the midlands. I can only describe the accent of the men from the Wirral as how the Irish would have sounded if they'd had better breeding, it wasn't English but it was closer than the chaps in the Emerald Isle. I was given the role of Squadron Commander, Number Three (Pennines) Company. A charming company of men, some of whom would easily fit into suburbia, if ambition ever took over them.

I settled into life at the Regiment rather well, my first duty was to take two weeks leave, after the stress of Northern Ireland I need to relax and recharge the old battery. So off I went to London and I stayed over at my old school chum 'growler' Barkers. The old dog hadn't changed he was still a character, still liked to drink the odd shot of whiskey and unfortunately, he still liked the rougher looking women.

To be fair he would have loved old butter face and by the amount Chugger drank, she would have liked him also.

The first evening there we went to a smashing little eatery they did a wonderful Grilled Aberdeen Angus sirloin steak béarnaise; except Growler being a bit of a drinker had his served with a red wine jus. We finished our repast and headed to one of the finer drinking establishments for champagne and ladies, not necessarily in that order. We weren't disappointed either, the champagne was outstanding and some of the damsels were of the highest order. Comtes De Champagne Taittinger 1988, highly recommended, a vintage worth every penny. Growler had just received a bonus from his employer in the region of two million pounds sterling so he wasn't shy buying the champagne. In his defence the award was fair after all he had been working at the company over two years, you can't buy that sort of loyalty; and the losses he made were rather small, compared to some other banks.

I met a charming young thing that night Naomi a Mediterranean looking thing. Slender curves in the right places and a backside high and firm, the sort of backside one would see in a tame rap video. I entertained her with my stories of frontline conflict, to moisten her up a little, get her juices flowing, we sipped a couple of bottles of bubbly to help the evening run along smoothly. Later I took Naomi to Growlers, for a cocktail and some frisky fun. Luckily for me she didn't disappoint. I allowed Naomi to explore my physique with her smooth tongue before I serviced her in a more continental position, as opposed to the usual missionary which was the style at university. After what seemed like minutes, I had poured my love into her and was left feeling the glow of success. I don't want to be crude, but I also gave her the honour of a second round the next morning, obviously she did the bulk of the work, I was tired, but this enabled her to leave with a womanly glow and a spring in her step, the lucky moo.

  I stayed at Growlers for a further few days before I got restless feet and moved on. I went back to the house and settled down for a relaxing few day. I met up with a young lady friend of the family Clara, a debutant studying English literature at Bath a pleasant girl, her father went to school with Uncle Rupert, we spent the evening drinking Port and I explained to her how I was awarded several medals, before we retired to the bedroom. It was there that Clara became nervous and explained to me how she was not yet a real woman. Ha the crazy fool I reassured her that it wasn't an issue and I would be gentle in taking her flower. Some ladies are rather nervous about losing their virginity, but as I always say, it is curable.

We crawled into bed and without a moment notice I made Clara a real woman, using several positions I had heard about from some of the working-class squaddies, I took her to womanhood with a vengeance, I dabbled in several positions, as sweat poured from me, such was the vigour of my performance and then I gracefully arrived over her, leaving her looking like a tradesman's radio. The following morning when I woke, I saw Clara laying there in the bed, looking dishevelled and worn, she her body ravished and tossed aside. It was at that point I felt a touch of sadness and yes dare I say guilt, as she woke up, I took her in my arms and gently wiped the hair from her face, I gently spoke and said "Clara my lovely little thing, I, with all my heart apologies for last night, but I had to stop, I was tired." She I believe wept a little as my words danced on her charming ears. Later we sat in bed talking and I explained that the previous evening was a one off although she was now of woman and a lovely filly, due to her studying at a second-rate university the relationship could not last. She took the news well and we remain friends to this day.

The following night I sat round the table with Uncle Sebastian and Father, we drank the evening away talking about life, the Saint Pauls first XV and the advantages and disadvantages of allowing Commonwealth citizens into the British Military. A joyful evening and one I still remember fondly, despite Uncle Sebastian's outburst vis-à-vis Fijians in his former regiment.

The reason I remember the evening fondly is simply because the next morning whilst eating Eggs Benedict, I was disturbed by the horrendous sound of an ambulance approaching the house. Uncle Sebastian had woken earlier that morning complaining of chest pains and a dull ache in his left arm. After father had debated with himself which hospital would be better suited to Uncle Sebastian's needs and finished his morning courgette with ricotta pomegranate and parsley oil on flatbread, he completed the Times crossword then bravely summoned an ambulance. Unfortunately, despite the best efforts of the hospital Uncle Sebastian was pronounced dead on arrival. A sad day for all and one that will be remembered by the local golf club for many years as Uncle Sebastian was a member there for many years.

Uncle Sebastian left behind him three ex-wives and a Labrador, he never had children, despite his best efforts no matter how many times he tried he could not get his low sperm count to impregnate a single wife. According to Jenna his first wife, he would rigorously service her in every position he could think of and no avail. It was such a shame because Uncle Sebastian would have made a wonderful father, on a positive note though as I was the only one from a younger generation, he left me all his belongings.

I sold his house immediately as I felt a seven bedroomed house in Surrey was not necessary for me and with his savings and insurance policy the thirteen million I inherited would be a nice nest egg for me. His latest lady friend was none too pleased but they hadn't married so she had no claim on Uncle Sebastian and at twenty-two years of age she still had a couple of years in her to bag herself a gentleman.

The funeral for Uncle Sebastian was not much fun. Firstly, his ex-wives would not stop showing emotion, Helen arrived with Sara and a young girl called Debbie, all three ladies dressed in black which was respectful, the collar Debbie was wearing not so much. However, as Sara pointed out, Helen liked a young lady in a collar, so I suppose it some fashion accessory that the ladies were wearing. Sara was looking fine and I believed if it wasn't such a sad occasion, I may have given her a reminder of the pleasure she once felt under me,

It was the first time I had met my Uncle Walter he turned up to the funeral, father and Walter had a cold relationship due to Walter joining the Navy, but the day was not about either man it was about Uncle Sebastian. He was laid to rest in the same plot as Uncle Rupert whom had departed this realm years earlier. Once the service was over, it was back to the house for some good old-fashioned Port and a spot of lunch.

It was during lunch that I spoke with Uncle Walter now Vice Admiral Thatcher CBE, it transpired he wasn't the sort I imagined, for one he had a strong eye for the ladies, and was rather crude with his terminology for a lady and her regions. A lovely chap, shame her let the family down.

I returned to my Regiment, relieved from the sexual accomplishments and financially secure due to the sad loss of Uncle Sebastian etc. My time within a Cavalry unit was fun, I didn't have to walk anywhere as the vehicles we used could be driven straight to the officer's mess, saving me time and energy. I had a new 'bat man' Trooper Holmes, he was from the Wirral however, he wasn't afflicted with the accent so that was a bonus. He was a typical young, urban man. A little rough round the edges and like many on a council estate he was heavily tattooed. But he could clean boots better than most, and he served a mean 'Irish' coffee. Living near Liverpool he probably had connections to Ireland, most of them seem to.

Going on exercise with a cavalry regiment was more fun that with the foot soldiers of the infantry, mainly as we drove everywhere. One particular exercise we took place in was a great time for me. After the first night under the stars, I realised how dull camping was so I arranged to spend the next evening in a local hotel. I got Trooper Holmes to book me the room, not one hundred per cent sure if I ever paid him back, anyway, he wouldn't mind time moves on and he would have only spent the money on alcohol and low-class women. My point ah, yes, well that evening whilst in the hotel's restaurant I was enjoying an exquisite braised pig cheek, pomme puree, charcutiere sauce. When I noticed my old friend Pinkie dining at another table with some friends of his. After finishing my meal, I went over and joined Pinkie, he introduced me to Sebastian, Juliane, Claire, Morrice and Nadine. A lovely bunch of people. Pinkie was comical, he had some charming terms of endearment for his friends, he introduced Claire as a Gillette Blade, apparently this is because she cuts both ways. I don't know what that means, I also discovered she was bi sexual, an interesting challenge there for old Bulldog I thought to myself, she was a fine-looking girl, shoulder length hair, and a glint in her eye, that spelled trouble, I liked her.

Sebastian was a charming man, five feet five inches tall and very muscular apparently a Friend of Dorothy, not sure who Dorothy was as she never turned up. Then there was Nadine an adorable strumpet. She was working with Pinkie and the gang in Theatre production, a charming lady former student of Gordonstoun an outstanding school, she later read History at Oxford. She was the most beautiful woman I had seen, granted she had the ubiquitous Gordonstoun long flowing blonde hair, she stood some five feet eleven, stunning blue eyes and a smile that made me twitch in my desired area I must admit to being smitten by this filly. She was educated and from one of the finer families in England. I found her to be beautiful, articulate and when I was speaking to her, I noticed a gentle her class, her style and my erection.

I spent the evening speaking with Pinkie and the gang and I had had an enjoyable time, unfortunately I did have a Squadron of men to lead the following morning and so I had to say a fond farewell to the guys. Before leaving I exchanged communication numbers with Nadine and arranged to meet her the following weekend.

The following week I had the men busy clean uniforms and polishing tanks. As the exercise was over and some of our equipment needed a good shine. I was rather disappointed in some of the men, it took them a whole two days to polish a tank to the standard I required. However luckily for them I had love on my mind.

Love

The following weekend I had arranged an evening out with the lovely Nadine. I arrived at the restaurant some five minutes earlier to ensure my suit was up to a presentable standard, my shoes where shining bright after Trooper Holmes had spent the day polishing them for me. I was wearing the regimental tie and without sounding brash I looked like a gentleman of the highest possible order.

   Nadine arrived fashionably two minutes late, ha, ladies and their traditions, they do amuse me. She looked exquisite, in a lovely blue dress that made her eyes light up several counties, her blonde hair flowing subtly in the breeze and a pair of heels that complemented her superlative legs. We sat and chatted whilst enjoying Beef Fillet Steak served with:

Portobello Mushroom Gratin, Sun Blushed Plum Tomato, Peppercorn Sauce. Nadine being a lady allowed me to order for her and she was served Pan Fried Cod, Broccoli Puree, Soya Beans, Pancetta Lardons, Beurre Blanc Sauce. We chatted and she told me all about her family, their wealth, education and their fine standing in the City. Her father worked for one of the finer banks in the world, her youngest brother was with the Foreign and Commonwealth Office, she also had a sister also in banking, I assumed in a secretarial role.

A true upstanding family. I of course told her in depth about my family and our links to the military. I gave Nadine a rub down of my exploits as an officer and we shared a joke or two about working with people from poorer backgrounds. It was a smashing evening, and the company was simply outstanding.

Later that evening I escorted Nadine to her million-pound London home and graciously, gave her a kiss good evening and a firm slap of her buttocks before bidding her good night.

I spent many a day back at the barracks day dreaming of young Nadine and her firm buttocks, how one day I would ride them like a knight returning triumphantly back from battle. I was smitten and by golly I fear love was raising its head.

The chaps within the squadron were somehow running along smoothly without me, discipline and military training at its best. Such was my style leadership that my men, developed a mind of their own and could solve problems without hassling me.

A few weeks later it was date four that I went to Nadine's London home and spent an evening talking and drinking enchanting wine, that evening Nadine looked splendid her hair tide back, she was wearing casual attire which was probably more suited for a gymnasium than a home, but it was a casual evening so I kept quiet. I myself had dressed down, in a pressed white shirt, regimental tie, but no blazer.

  Later in the evening we moved the discussion to the business of sexual relations. I was frankly shocked by Nadine's open and honest approach. She openly admitted to being pure of physical love, however, she had indulged and had vast experience of love with a battery powered stimulus. I assured her that this still meant she was pure and that her standing in society would not be affected.

  I took it upon myself to remove my garments and suggest making love, within the confines of the living room. Nadine joined me in removing her casual attire, her beautiful body on display making me emotionally and physically aroused; we consummated our love there and then on the shag pile. Our bodies entwined, moving as one, our fluids merging together to form a tsunami of juices.

   That was it, Bulldog was in love. All it took was the firm thighs of a lady, the fragrance of mating and the flowing of fluids between two highly educated people. I knew there and then that I would marry this lucky lady. The look she gave me as she gently wiped her lower lip after pleasuring my man handle told me this was a lady that I could spend many years with.

   The next morning, I dashed back to the Regiment, I went straight to my office and after Trooper Holmes had served me an English Breakfast tea, I penned a letter on regimental letter headed paper to Nadine's father. Requesting that he allow me to marry his daughter. I dispatched Trooper Homes away immediately to deliver the note. Granted in the note I was a little abrupt, however Bulldog had got the scent.

  Within the hour I had received a telephone call from Nadine's father. After exchanging pleasantries and discussing Fathers recent golf trip, Nadine's father gave me permission to take his daughter in wed lock and he explained how he was extremely proud that our two families would join together in union. He accepted my apology for the blunt note, he assured me he understood that passion sometimes make a man do things he regrets.

  Nadine's father swiftly arranged a gathering at his family estate, for both families to celebrate the news. I know Nadine was going to be excited when she found out about the forthcoming engagement. Nadine's father lived in a tasteful seventeenth century manor, only the twelve bedrooms. However, it was tastefully decorated, many of the trophies and animal skins coming from all corners of the globe.

The evening of the engagement I presented at Nadine's house; Trooper Holmes had pressed and delivered my clothes earlier that day. Father was there, proud and glowing, his dinner jacket pressed to perfection, his medals gleaming. I think by the look he gave me, there was pride in his eyes. Either that or his cataracts had returned. Nadine's father Raymond, was wearing a stunning dinner jacket for the occasion he was stood proud speaking with father, both men looked happy and educated as they sipped their whiskey and joked about holidays they shared as children together in the South of France.

Helen was there with Sara, both ladies wearing stunning if not rather tight-fitting dresses, I assumed they were nervous of such a high-profile event as they stood there holding hands and giggling, I personally would not wear leather to an engagement party, but the dress suited Helen.

I went to Nadine's room and was greeted a sight of beauty, she wore a stunning red dress, that sat right in all the correct places. Her hair was immaculate and her make-up subtle but arousing, her legs delicately wrapped in silk stocking, glowing in the early evening sunset. She was a picture of heaven; Bulldog was both in love and aroused in equal parts.

I took her hand and explained that the evening was to celebrate our engagement. I at this point took out a white gold ring and lowered onto one knee and said "princess, will you do me the honour of becoming my future wife, my lover and if required my friend, will you honour your fathers word, as he has already promised you to me" Nadine of course said yes, typically as ladies do she became a tad emotional and kissed me, but what the hell it was a special occasion, a single tear ran down her perfect porcelain face, just the right amount of emotion for an educated lady.

We posed for photographs from a leading celebrity magazine, such is the nature of engagements and weddings. In correct society a family does not pay for their own marriage, that would be ridiculous. We instead invited a society magazine, and ensured many a socialite and military leader were present.

Bothe families were happy when we presented in the main hall and Nadine flashed her ring, to gasps from the crowd. It sparkled and lit up the room. The evening was a smashing occasion many friends and family attended. Pinkie brought Sebastian along, still no sign of his friend Dorthey, 'Sawdust' and 'Growler' attended with what I assumed were female guests. Champagne flowed and the conversations were appropriate It was a stunning evening that finished with Nadine and myself together joined as one; Nadine riding me like she was a dressage champion*.

_{It being an engagement party I insisted Nadine kept her stocking on, mainly as I was tired and the sight of her dressed in only stockings, made my arrival, somewhat swift.}

The next day I arrived back at the regiment, the Sergeants Mess had a whip round and bought me a lovely lead decanter complete with regimental crest for my engagement, , the Officers Mess presented me a silver statue Lady Thatcher proudly laughing at the Miners, and the ordinary ranks presented me with a painting of the family crest. To rampant lions stood on a crown. The with motto 'Et cum

Magnifico splendor oriri.' 'I rise with magnificent splendour.' It was a pleasant start to the day. I thanked all concerned and then ordered the men, to practice their drill, as I would be requiring a company of men to be at my wedding to present a guard of honour and of course some lower ranks to act as waiters and orderlies.

As it was going to be such a prestigious occasion, I cancelled all leave.

The commanding officer called me into the office, firstly to congratulate me on engaging with such an impressive piece of skirt and to announce that I had been promoted to the rank of major. I was honoured at the news and ordered my bat man to present my uniforms with the new rank insignias before evening meal. A task that would take him a mere four hours and a task he was more than up to. I myself was exhausted after such a morning so I took a well-deserved nap.

Life was running smoothly, I had a promotion, a lady of good order, good friends and the love of the men within the regiment. So, I took two weeks leave. There was nothing I could do within the regiment as the men were marching all day, so Pinkie arranged for a quick boating trip to the Med.

On the boat, Marins Saucy (*saucy seamen*) there was Pinkie, Sebastian, Growler, Sawdust, Ja'quan and Philippe, the latter being friends of Pinkie. Both great chaps, muscular in a tasteful way and both had a wicked sense of humour. It was a stunning vessel loaned to Pinkie by a friend he had made at the BBC, Pinkie wouldn't say who the friend was, except if I watched the news, I would work it out.

We sailed down to Spain and dropped anchor, we spent most of the days swimming, Pinkie and Ja'quan introduced me to something called skinny dipping. Which is basically men stripping and then swimming in the sea. It seemed rather continental and as I always say when in Venice. I would say when in Rome but it has become a little too commercialised for me, now that discount airlines are available the working classes, anyway they have the right to visit anywhere. Also, with the Vatican being in Rome, well Catholics everywhere. Nothing against them I adhere to the no condom rule every time. But all that assumption on everything being a sin. Please, how can having a few dinkies or smoking a fine Cuban with a lady of the night be a sin? So, as I say when in Venice do as the Romans. Pinkie loved to parade au natural and so did his friends which I found a little strange, Pinkie's friends hadn't been to public school so being naked around chaps must be a novel past time. But they took to it with ease, and for that I salute them.

After a week of drinking, skinny dipping and chasing the boys around the boat in a playful manner I headed back to the regiment. Pinkie, Growler and the boys stayed on the yacht for a couple of more weeks. By all account's Growler was very popular with Ja'quan. But that was Growler all over, he could take any situation and just suck it up.

Back at the regiment the men were looking smart and presentable, ready for their duties at my forthcoming nuptials. The men had spent weeks polish boots and pressing uniforms, the standard of drill was up there with the Household Division and my bat man had arranged my uniforms correctly.

The week before the wedding the men of my company arranged what the poor call a 'stag do' or a gentleman's weekend if you are raised correctly.

We met by the guard room and headed into town. In the first bar, a strange place called The Golden Cock we were greeted by scantily clad 'ladies' many from such jobs as cleaners or factory workers. Their choice of clothing seemed to be imitation PVC legging, a tight top and enough make up for a netball team.

  Their drink of choice would be bright blue and consumed directly from the bottle. The music was loud and of a rather camp nature. But the men enjoyed it. I endured a pint of cider and indulged in idle chat with some of the men. I found them to be quite interesting, for example one of the Troopers actually left school with GCSE's, seven to be precise. He came from a council estate, obviously only one parent, but he managed to work hard and gain qualifications. I was astounded and yet rather proud of this chap. Maybe a candidate for a promotion, in the future. What I did find confusing was the number of chaps raised by just the one parent. Was this because working class people use IVF, or are the women so foul that the men impregnate them and move on. I wasn't sure but either way I was having a pleasant evening and these chaps had dragged themselves out of a council estate, so they deserved limited success in life.

It was about nine in the evening when I was feeling a little delicate after consuming cider, lager, bitter and several spirits, that the boys played a prank on me the old devils. I was ambushed outside the Golden Cock public house I was debagged and strapped to a lamp post. Despite my cries for help I was left there as the men went on to another bar. I was stood at the lamp post wearing just a pair of socks, for what seemed like several hours, before a passing police vehicle rescued me. Unfortunately for me, I was placed under arrest and taken to the local police station, they tried to claim I was Drunk and Disorderly, also something to do with exposing myself as my rigid member was on view to members of the public.

For nearly an hour I was in that police station, before a friend of mine 'K9' came to my rescue. K9 or to give her, her correct title Michaela Van Der Horne QC. We called her K9 as she had some amazing puppies. Anyway, Michaela was outraged at my treatment she demanded to speak with the Chief Superintendent a charming fellow and Michaela's uncle. He was astonished to see me in his station and found the whole charges to be laughable. He scolded the arresting officer in front of us, explaining to the man, how our families were interconnected K9 was a second cousin of mine, he brother Luke went to St Pauls before he was tragically run over by fathers Bentley leaving him with a permeant limp, the family rightly disowned him and he hasn't been spoken about since, it was explained to the officer how a British gentleman having hijinks is part of the upper-class privilege and that arresting a major of the British Army was at best irresponsible. I was released immediately with an apology.

I thanked K9 and informed her of how I was looking forward to seeing her at the wedding. The next morning many of the men were feeling the negative side of alcohol, so I had the Physical Training team run them, before they continued with their drill lessons.

Before anyone knew it the day of my wedding was approaching with great speed. I went to Fathers the night before the wedding and stayed in the house, to prepare for my big day. Helen and Sara were at the house, both girls were rather excitable and I dare say giddy, both girls were having a massage from two friends of they had staying over Kelly and Claire, charming girls, and they never once complained overtly regarding the leather outfits they had to wear to perform their duties. The massages must have lasted a while as I saw both girls leave the next morning. I stayed in the house, I drank some wine, and had my last session masturbating as a single man, and unfortunately my last ever session masturbating, as from the following day I would have a lady to perform those duties for me. I remember as I sat, there in the arm chair, raised penis in hand thinking how at the age of fifteen I had first ridden solo at St Pauls, spending many nervously hours playing a game of soggy biscuit with the chaps. Back then I was a shy boy, nervously trying not to be the last one to erupt on the biscuit, for I firmly disliked a custard cream and I therefore didn't want to have to eat it. Here I was years later my final heave before I retired in the sport of one-handed javelin. It was a sad day after an illustrious career, but a rather enjoyable finale.

The following morning, my bat man arrived and my immaculate uniform was presented to me, after a shower and of course my bat man had shaved me, I dressed. Without sounding too self-important, when I looked into the mirror, I looked astonishing, dressed in my No1 uniform, my medals gleaming. As I stood there and admired the view, I felt a prang of guilt, for technically it was Nadine's day and there was no chance of her looking this good. Within moments of me admiring myself, the butler came into my quarters and announced the arrival of my good friend Chugger Peters, he was serving with the Royal Air Force at the time, he arrived wearing his RAF uniform, granted he looked smart and on any other day he would have been the smartest person in the room, but this was Bulldogs day and Peters looked sort of average. We dismissed the bat man, and we went downstairs, got into the Bentley and drove to the church.

As we got there It was a splendid sight, the boys from school were there, Sawdust, Growler, Non sense Kelly. Some of my former conquests were present, Claudia, Sara, Tamara, all looking radiant, dressed to a high standard; K9 was there wearing a stunning dress, figure hugging allowing ample view of the puppies. It reminded me of the day I allowed her to folate me on her father's estate, to this day the only girl to ever insert a digit into me to enhance my arrival.

Jessica and father were present, smiling as I approached, Father smiled and informed me of how proud my mother would have been if it not for her untimely, and somewhat accidental death, moving words from a proud man, who refused to show emotion. Helen was present, she wore a beautiful pastel summer dress, although short and tight it was still classy. It must have presented problems with ironing as Sara spent many a moment smoothing the dress on Helens backside, such a lovely caring girl to worry about Helens outfit.

Inside the church I waited, for Nadine, as the clock struck three, I wanted to leave as I couldn't believe Nadine was late, but Peters pointed out, it is a ladies prerogative to be late on her wedding day, and thirty seconds was not too long for a gentleman to wait. I know I should have left but I assume I was caught up in the romance. With a few seconds Nadine arrived. So, I internally forgave her. Nadine looked mind-blowingly beautiful. Her hair was perfection, he make-up minimal but lighting her face up, her dress was ivory and fitted like a glove, her stockings subtle and glossy, as I had requested. She looked beautiful and came a very close second to how good I looked.

We went through the necessary stuff which you have to do, Nadine, as tradition and I dictated promised to Love Honour and Obey, writing your own vows are for working class people whom assume they are middle class. I promised to love her etc. to be honest I wasn't listening. The vicar pronounced us man and wife, I gave Nadine a firm kiss on the cheek and walked down the aisle to polite applause. We walked through the guard of honour and off we went for a six-course meal and plenty of champagne. Before I consummated our union, insisting Nadine kept on the stockings and veil, just to make it slightly erotic but not overly kinky, not on such an occasion.

  That evening our guest indulged in the champagne fuelled social event of the season. We danced, we laughed, we spoke about old times and we enjoyed each other's company.

  Bulldog and Nadine, it had a beautiful ring to it, we were young, happy, sexually active and now married. We were the Clintons of British society, however, unlike the Clintons, I would never expel my love on a lady's dress, after satisfying her I would want her to absorb my juices not some material.

Kosovo

Within days of my wedding news broke out, the regiment was to once again travel to foreign places and serve NATO. When I say days after my wedding apparently the order came through just before the wedding but I was too busy to read orders and information. Luckily one of my lieutenants had, and the men were ready to go. It was with some sadness I was going to have to say good bye to my wife, she had become a firm favourite of mine and the evening nuptials had become a part of my night time routine. But duty calls, and not all duties are enjoyable ones.

The evening prior to leaving I said goodbye to Nadine, and she serviced my gentleman's area with her tongue and mouth as a parting gift. Before I left for the barracks, I gently gave her firm backside a spank smiled and went on my way. Once back at the barracks I consulted a map and discovered I was in fact going to the former Yugoslavia not near India as I first believed Kosovo to be. I gathered the men and gave them a rousing speech for them to take comfort from.

Gentlemen, yet again the world has looked to me and my regiment. Again, we are expected to travel to foreign parts and protect the innocent, yet again we will stand tall and show how the British keep the peace and defend our interests around the world. We will endeavour to travel out as one unit and come back as one unit. We may take casualties along the way and we may have to bury one or two of you. this gentleman is the reality of being a British hero, at times it is difficult and so it should be, for what would an army be if it were simply marching, polishing uniforms and impressing the civilian ladies? I understand that many of you haven't had the opportunity to wish your loved ones well, what with training for, then performing at my wedding, but again duty comes before everything. Finally, gentlemen remember when we are out there, we are British we are the 74th (Edward the VIII Own) Dragoons and we are children of Her Majesty the Queen.

God speed.

Yet again I pulled it out of the hat, a speech for the men to devour, one that will fill them with pride and one that will allow them to carry out their duties with pride, to be honest I believe I may have had an erection whilst giving the speech, for it was that powerful. I got my batman print the speech and present it to the junior ranks mess.

The morning of our departure arrived. We travelled to Brize Norton in convoy, me taking up the rear as an officer should. On arrival, I spent a few short hours in the officer's mess enjoying a dram of whisky whilst the men loaded our equipment. Before departing for Kosovo.

When we arrived at the heavily bombed country, I realised what a tough job we had, I was aware the US was using Kosovo for bombing target, I just never realised how good the United States Air Force actually were.

Our unit was tasked with intelligence, surveillance and reconnaissance, based at the force's headquarters, in the Kosovan capital, Pristina. On the first day I decided I would accompany the men on a quick drive around town. We jumped into the vehicles and drove around, the first thing to strike me was, the place was a dump, secondly the fillies weren't overly blessed in the looks department, luckily as a married man, I didn't need the help of a young filly so it wasn't too much a problem.

I decided to have a go myself at driving an armoured vehicle and being in such a hellish place seemed like a place to start. I felt the power of the engine as I forced the vehicle to full speed, and the yelp of enjoyment by the troop sergeant as I ragged it around a corner, I was starting to enjoy myself. Unfortunately, the blighter doesn't handle as well as a Bentley and as I accelerated around the corner, they bloody thing toppled over. Luckily, we all managed to scramble out and no foul was committed. It took the chaps from the Royal Electrical and Mechanical Engineers a couple of hours to recover the scimitar but those chaps enjoy those sorts of jobs. And luckily for me I managed to get one of the junior officers to drive me back to camp in time for a smashing evening meal of Hay Aged Bresse Duck, Smoked Beetroot and Lavender. So, in all a good day.

  My second time on patrol some two weeks late I came across some unfriendly fighters from the Kosovo Liberation Army. They were being brutish and I found them to be ill trained and without manners. I approached their senior man and explained to him my views. He replied something to me in foreign and I quite rightly took offence. I explained to him in no uncertain terms that his attitude would result in me shooting him, his dog, and the rest of his troops, he soon retreated. My men once we had moved away and made their weapons safe were extremely proud of my actions. It was the last time the Company Sergeant Major asked me to attend a patrol with the men, I think my style of leadership made him feel inadequate, I for one was glad not to go off camp again, it was a vile place.

  The following day I received a dispatch from Regimental Headquarters praising me for my action and stating I had been put forward for the Queens Gallantry Medal, it was of course a formality as Dickie and father were close chums with 'Randy' Smith-Western in the Cabinet Office. Also, Dickie had put me forward for the award as he had promised father, he would look out for me. It was a great start to the day for myself and the men, I paraded them that morning and told them the news. Their little red faces will stay with me for many a year.

Following on from receiving the QGM I decided that my style of leadership was more office based and the Company Sergeant Major could not agree quick enough, therefore I was leading from my office using up to date technology and of course briefings from the young officers.

The entire tour was becoming a chore so I requested to return to England, after the twenty-eight days, which guaranteed me a medal. My request was granted and I returned to my unit, and the ample breasts of my wife, I was so excited to be back I dashed home and with vigour and passion and entered via the back door. Nadine was surprised, but happy when I entered and took it upon herself to drop to her knees and embrace the conquering hero.

I went to my office every day to read emails and check up on my men, by all accounts they were managing very well with my unique, distancing approach to management. In the afternoons I would go to the Officers' Mess and enjoy a whisky and a chat, before going home and servicing Nadine in our matrimonial home.

Grief

One afternoon I had just finished a robust ménage a deux with my wife, when I received a call from Helen. She sounded upset and although this annoyed me, I accepted it when she told me the news that father had sadly passed away on a shooting holiday with the regimental association. He had been out in the morning shooting grouse, later that day he was indulging in a cocaine fuelled romp with Jessica when his ticker suddenly stopped. Jessica was close to climax and rather alarmed when father stiffened up and died. Leaving her a widow and unfulfilled sexually, with a fourteen stone stiff laying on her

I took the news well, as a gentleman and officer, I had no choice I simply had Nadine make me Grilled Kippers, before I left for the family house.

On arrival at the house, I quickly had the butler move Jessica's belonging to the cottage that Helen was using, the two girls would have to share with each other, Sara and Sara's new friend Mandy. Jessica's took the news well, I assume she took it well, one could hardly tell, with her outbursts of grief and her pointless use of crying. It wouldn't bring father back, nor allow the orgasm father had denied her earlier that morning.

I called on Pinkie as he somehow knew interior designers and within the hour, he arrived with Ja'quan and a designer named Jean Paul Chatte a respectable designer from Pays de la Loire region of France. Together Jean Paul and Ja'quan came up with new designs for each room. And gave me a guarantee they would be finished for my moving in. For gentlemen, both had a good eye for colour and design, they amazed me with their knowledge or colours, shades and pastels.

  I arranged Fathers funeral with the help of his Regimental Headquarters, they sorted out the church, the service running order, dates and times, I arranged for champagne to be delivered. It was a stressful time, but I managed to get through it. The day of the funeral arrived. I was woken early that morning, by Nadine, she had dressed suitably, black stockings, black thong and black dress, her backside presenting like a ripe peach in a silk handkerchief. My bat man had cleaned my shoes and pressed my suit. I dressed and waited for the formalities to begin. Before I knew where I was the cars had arrived myself and Nadine drove from the barracks to fathers, well now my house, Jessica, Sara and Helen were present all three ladies dressed in black as is tradition, Helens dress again was a little tight and short but it is what father would have wanted. We drove to the church, we were greeted by many of father's friends and ex-lovers, men from his former regiment were there to carry the coffin. I couldn't be bothered with standing around so I went and took my seat in the church. Before long, fathers' body was brought in, the vicar said some kind words, regarding father, his outstanding military career, his wives, his love of golf his passion for high priced escorts and of course myself. Father was then brought back to the estate to be buried in a private ceremony. Fathers lead lined coffin was carried by six men from the regimental, the look of pain on their faces showed they respect they had for him as a man.

Father was laid to rest and we went back to the house as the butler back filled the grave.

In the house we chatted about days gone by and scraps father had gotten into. I spoke with the family solicitor to ensure all the relevant paper work was in order. I was to receive the house, eight million pound and all fathers' belongings. Helen was to receive one million pounds and Jessica alike received one million pounds. When I informed Helen of the news her reaction shocked me to the core. She turned to Sara and said 'darling we are rich' I despise the Nuevo rich, when I enquired to her remarks, she informed me that herself and Sara we engaged in a sexual relationship and were in fact lesbians. I swear to the good lord I almost dropped my champagne. How could this be the case? Helen had never given any clues, for a start she had long hair and wore make-up. She didn't like men's sports and she wore dresses. Sara was once a lover of mine, yes it made sense she would remove herself to lesbia, as once having slept with me no other man would please her in such a manner again.

   Pinkie assured me that Helen and Sara being gay was not an issue and I should accept them as they are. Pinkie was wise and understood the gay community, such a caring sole he is. I assured Helen I was fine with her being of the lesbian persuasion and I forgave Sara, for turning. I explained they would always be welcome to live in the cottage on the estate, well I did so after consulting Dr Lincoln our family GP and he assured me neither I nor Nadine could catch homosexuality. Helen was grateful with the news; she was a little bit put out when I explained I did not understand lesbian relations and asked if I could watch one day to grasp an understanding, however she didn't say no.

Also present at father's funeral was Sir Michael Davis-Hope KBE, DSO a lovely man, he'd been a friend of fathers since they were young chaps at the Military Academy. Sir Michael, told me anecdotes of him and father chasing skirt and drinking heavily in the old days, during the cold war, they would spend many a night with ladies from Germany indulging in European style love making. Sir Michael then offered to have me transferred to Whitehall as he explained, I had suffered enough with Northern Ireland, Bosnia, Kosovo and working with chaps from the north.

I with a heavy heart travelled back to my regiment the next day, I got the entire company to parade and I explained that I would with immediate effect be leaving the Regiment. This was greeted by the tradition one cheer, that the Regiment adopted whenever I gave them news, I assumed it was three cheers rolled into one, the noise the men made. Sadden by my parting.

  I arranged for my bat man to be allowed back into a troop to continue his work within the regiment. After he had packed and shipped my belongings. I turned and walked out of the regiment, I didn't look back, the noise of the men, happily going about their duties, told me they would be fine. I left and headed home. There heavy of heart I for one last time allowed Nadine to folate me in the Regimental home. Before moving on to Whitehall and the family estate.

  Moving into the house was strange, Ja'quan and Jean Paul had remodelled the house, Pinkie loved it. The colours would not have been my choosing but they worked, the kitchen was modern white with the walls painted labia pink' a stunning shade of pink. My study had all my books on a new shelving unit designed by Ja'quan and the walls painted a beautiful shade Ja'quan assure me it was called 'starfish mocha', I adored it, a rather modern feel, but still maintaining the classic English country house look, they even took into account my military bearings, by painting the walls of the staircase a sea man white, the place was bourgeois and imagined, both myself and Nadine adored it.

  At the house Nadine was quiet, but quieter than a lady should be. I took her by the hand and said pumpkin tell old 'Bulldog' what is on your female brain, she wept slightly and informed me she was with child. Granted she would lose her figure and her vagina would never be as tight again, but this was good news. The family name would survive and move forward another generation. I immediately phoned St Pauls and put the child's name down for schooling, a god school always has a waiting list. Then Nadine shocked me to the core, she explained, placing a child's name down at St Pauls may be a little premature as there was at least a forty per cent chance the child could be born female.

The horror never entered my head, but of course, there was always that possibility that an unborn offspring could be female. I must be truthful and say that news knocked me for six, but after some smelling salts and a swift brandy I thought about it logically, I remember the day we engaged in love making and the position we used was all pointing to us having a boy. But, a girl what harm could, a female Thatcher.do?

Ja'quan and Pinkie were so excited about the news, they popped some champagne and we drank until the early hours of the morning, before they left to go house hunting, or cottaging as they called it.

I phoned Tamara an old college friend and explained my wife would be with child for many months, as is the fashion and asked if she would be able to assist me with my inner fluids, as to be frank, making love to a fat lady, would be very difficult, not only because they are not attractive, even if they are carrying my child, there is also the logistics of it all. Tamara wasn't happy with my call, for some reason, I assumed it was the wrong time of the month to address her. Luckily Pinkie knew a girl whom according to Pinkie could suck start the Bentley. She sounded ideal, and a friendship was quickly established on a temporary basis you understand.

Whitehall

My first day at my new office saw me settling in and learning my new role. I had a secretary, an assistant and a very generous allowance for such necessities as, meal, travel and entertaining. All things that are essential for running the Ministry of Defence. The dining hall was a lovely place, I would be spending many hours there as Nadine was with child and therefore, not exactly what a man wants to look at whilst eating. My assistant was a pleasant young lady, she didn't attend a public school, but somehow managed to gain entry into one of the better universities. She had a grasp of politics and current affairs. And was easy on the eye, so all good as far as work was going. At home Nadine was ballooning, with child and displaying hormonal tendencies. I believe it is the 'miracle' of giving new life. Personally, I found it a bit of a chore.

Work was going well, I would attend meetings, discuss current political thinking and have my assistant crunch data for me. I was a fighting man; data was for ladies and accountants. The dining hall was where the powerful would sit and meet, a gentleman can get some important meetings completed whilst enjoying Ballotine of Duck Liver followed by Coconut Souffle with Vanilla Chantilly and Raspberries.

One of my duties was to augment combat capabilities of the Armed Forces by reducing wasteful expenditure. On paper this seems simple, get rid of the county certain regiments, of course I'm thinking the Welsh ones, they can join the Mercian Regiment, that's on the border with Wales one assumes, the Irish Regiments, give them to Dublin, maybe offer the odd Mick a job with a Scottish Regiment, they all sound the same anyway, of course disband the Parachute regiment, they never jump into battle and I always found the maroon beret a little bit ostentatious. However, the reality is slightly different, the Parachute Regiment are a good solid regiment, despite the beret. The Irish, well they love a good punch up and politically, getting rid of them was a big no no within the halls of power. Also, the Welsh, well, as Whitehall views it as a country they have to stay as well. So was not going to easy.

During my time at the Ministry of Defence I took up golf, never saw the point to be honest. Hitting a ball then walking after it, then hitting away from yourself again, but it got me out of the office. It was during one long walk that I had a brilliant idea. I called the regiment and had a new bat man sent down. Trooper Collins. Bloody good chap, fit as a whippet. He improved the game of golf no end. I would walk to the tee, launch the ball a few hundred metres and Trooper Collins would go and fetch it for me, save on walking. I would bang my balls up the fairway a couple of times, then get bored go to the club house and have a couple of whiskies. Troop Collins would return to the regiment, waiting on stand by for my next game. I really did start to enjoy the game.

I visited Saint Pauls to give a speech to the boys at the old school. Fine body of youth, strapping lads, in their prime. They were of course eager to meet me and listen to my stories of the troubles and NATO duties. I also managed to watch a smashing game, the Saint Pauls first XV, thrashing Harrow on the rugby pitch. A beautiful day.

It was during the latter part of the game that I received a message from Nadine, she had gone into labour and was for some reason expecting me to be there? I am sure being with child pickles a lady's brain.

I ordered my driver to fetch the car, and we drove to the hospital, on the way there I could not think for the life of me why I was needed. The driver claimed it was to witness the birth, but surely not, isn't that the responsibility of the mid wife? The doctor well he delivers the baby, and mid wives, witness it? What else would they be doing except standing around. I was informed that my wife had been admitted to the Chelsea and Westminster Hospital. I was beyond annoyed. Although a fine hospital, with dedicated staff. It was a National Health Service Hospital. My driver informed me that it had a private wing the Kensington Wing, how a working-class man would know this I don't know and it wasn't the time of the place. But I was not having my child born in a hospital with the lower classes I immediately, contacted Nadine and despite her late stages of labour, insisted she move to St. Mary's Hospital, west London. A private ambulance was arranged as she was moved. St Mary's being good enough for the royal family then it is good enough for my child.

When I arrived at the hospital, I was escorted to a lovely private room, were Nadine was dilated and in some discomfort. Unfortunately for me, when I entered the room, I caught a glimpse of the business end. I can assure you, that I have never to this date eaten chopped liver, and I never will. Nadine was making a scene, what with her making grunting noises and occasional groans. I apologised on several occasions to the staff for this, but they seemed to find unnecessary outburst acceptable? Her face was without make-up and her hair was ruffed, that was simply not acceptable. To be honest the whole event was a bit of a chore, so I found a room with a television and watched the cricket, whilst Nadine embarrassed the family name.

After a number of mind numbingly boring hours a doctor entered the room and announced that I had a daughter. It was a bit of a let-down after all that wait, but bless her she was my off spring and I would love her regardless of her genetic disadvantage. I went into the room, Nadine had calmed down, and thankfully made herself presentable, her hair was now combed and her make-up applied. The young child was in a cot, a nurse asked if I wanted to hold her, but I declined.

After all I was wearing full military uniform.

  We decided that our daughter would have the name of Elizabeth Victoria Thatcher. A beautiful name for a beautiful daughter. I spoke with the administration team at Gordonstoun and placed her name down for schooling, you can't mess around with your child's education, even a female. Life was going smoothly; Nadine was busy with a personnel trainer to remove the unsightly mass she had produced during her incubation period. And I had spoken with a leading expert with regards to her having her vagina tightened back to how it was prior to the birth. A gentleman should not fall into a swimming pool when he is used to mere paddling.

Iraq

Back at Whitehall news was quickly spreading through the corridors of power regarding a forth coming war with Iraq. Granted we had been there previously, however, we didn't finish the job, as at the time it was not politically correct to kill a vicious dictator whilst he was supplying us with cheap oil. However, now he had decided to stop using the Dollar as currency we could no longer turn a blind eye to his evil treatment of the Kurds some ten years earlier, after all they were his own people and any of his enemies now became our allies making our task somewhat easier. We had to stop funding his regime and finally take the moral high ground.

Papers were written and documents produced that clearly showed that Saddam Hussein was in possession of illegal chemical weapons. Granted he had never used them, nor displayed them, bought them, nor had any person ever witnessed, and none appeared during or after the war but that wasn't the point, he had them. Our experts told us of the dangers and we were to act accordingly. Our experts drew up documentation and reliable evidence that this man was evil, all but one agreed, but he went for a walk one afternoon and must have changed his mind, because for some unknown reason he went silent.

All planning had to change, we had to ensure all troops were ready for this battle, we had to ensure that reservists were on standby and ready to go. I quite admired the reservists, not real soldiers, but nearly as good, and if these men and women were prepared to leave their mundane jobs and fight for Her Majesty then they were good enough for me.

I went back to my old regiments, firstly the 2nd Battalion South Yorkshire and Derbyshire Fusiliers, I spoke with the commanding officer and gave him a brief outline of what was going to happen. His chef supplied a beautiful lunch of Anjou Pigeon with Celeriac, Spice Pear and Truffle. It really did take the edge off explaining expected casualty numbers. I wished Dickie well and best of wishes to the Regiment.

I then went to see the 74th (Edward VIII) Dragoons and spoke with the commanding officer, we had a lovely day, speaking about how the regiment would be deployed, how Harrow were no longer the force they once were on the rugby pitch and of course the fact that half the regiment may potentially not return from the war. The chef served up a beautiful Roast loin of venison with caramelised cauliflower braised red cabbage with blackcurrant sauce. I explained to the commanding officer that Mr Hussein was a vile and evil psychotic killer, and that as a result the 74th Dragoons would with immediate affect land in Iraq and head straight to oil fields to protect the production. I left wishing him and his men the very best of luck.

　Back at home Nadine was back to her normal beautiful self. The nanny we hired was doing a smashing job with Elizabeth, the family unit was charming and something I had begun to enjoy. The eve of the invasion, I took Nadine to the master bedroom and I indulged her, with love making, her vagina now being back to its normal pre-birth size. I decided on a different position to my usual, as on this occasion I wanted to impregnate her with a boy. It was a rather vigorous and speedy session as I was expected back in Whitehall. I planted my seed and bid

Nadine well, as I went off to fight for my country, from a bunker in a secret location, in England. Nadine although sexually satisfied and legs akimbo waved goodbye as I left the room.

In the heavily guarded secret underground bunker, I will admit, I felt a twinge of nervous excitement. I imagined how the men on the frontline, sat in the desert were feeling exactly the same. We were all fighting this war and we were all putting ourselves at risk. I spoke with the Chief of Defence staff and ensured that by directing the war we were still entitled to the same medal as everyone else involved, he assured me we would be and he pointed out as leaders, the honours system would also acknowledge our commitment. I settled in for the start of hostilities with a plain scone Cornish clotted cream, Marco Polo gelée. The horrors of war all around.

After the first day or two I found the whole war experience a little tedious and managed to find space in Whitehall to have a bed installed to allow for afternoon naps and visits form my Nanny, who as well as looking after Elizabeth, also took care of some of my needs. I wasn't being vulgar and having an affair, it was simply an arrangement whilst Nadine was with child, and it continued for only a few months afterwards. During combat a gentleman has to expel stress and with Nadine being busy, she couldn't always assist with such matters. Later when she announced she was again with child Nanny had to continue with her duties for me as like many a man I find large ladies offensive and sexually unattractive and grotesque.

The war was going according to plan, the British doing an astounding job, those oil fields were secured, the Americans, well, they were being

American over the top and rather brash. Nadine's pregnancy was moving along nicely. Although the pregnant form is not one, I admire, Nadine did look well whilst carrying my off spring, she had a glow, a sparkle, if only she wasn't plump.

As the bulk off the war passed and we were left with the more boring cleaning up duties Nadine finally came to an end of her pregnancy one Saturday evening, it was just after I had finished dinner, so I wasn't too put out by it all. My driver took us to the hospital and I settled in a waiting area, Nadine understood me not going into the delivery room. She remembered how long it took me to pleasure her with my tongue after Elizabeth was born. I settled in for the long slog, after Nadine's reconstructive surgery her vagina was as good as a childless lady. However, as look would have it, out popped another off spring in no time. It was like a wet rugby ball slipping from muddy hands.

  On this occasion the gods were smiling down on old Bulldog, an heir was produced a strapping young boy, the news was amazing. I could not believe my luck, making Nadine lay on the bed legs akimbo after relations paid off. Into the world entered Montgomery Winston Thatcher.

  I spoke on the telephone to the Head of Saint Pauls and bagged Monty a place in the lower school when he turns seven. Then I dashed down to the Wellington Club to meet the men. I had my driver text message Nadine to offer congratulations, and I believe he ordered flowers for her, very thoughtful gesture.

  At the club, the boys were there, Growler, Sawdust, Nonsense, Chugger. From the military there was Striker, from the Fusiliers, Bucky from the Dragoons and Whitewash from

Whitehall, lovely fella in charge of data, hence the name. We celebrated with Veuve Clicquot Ponsardin Vintage, as it was lunchtime. It was from there we trotted off for a spot of lunch a magnificent Fresh Pasta with Braised Short Rib Ragu. Then on for some Dom Perignon, 1996 Champagne, in Kensington. Before stopping off Dow's, 1955 vintage Port. Highly recommended, extraordinarily fresh, powerful; very fine and focused. Was a splendid afternoon. Most of the chaps left, however, myself, Pinkie and Ja'quan headed out to K9s house, as she was having a merriment of her own, something to do with a birthday or something. Regardless of what the event I was celebrating the news every man wants to hear, I had a son.

  The next morning, I woke, feeling somewhat, I woke feeling a little delicate and rather confused I was not in my normal bed, or the bed of my mistress. I was in a large room, en suite, with pastel shades wallpaper, obviously the room of a lady. As I rolled over, to my surprise and horror laying there was K9, her puppies heaving in the morning sunlight. I didn't know if one should be shocked or surprised. K9 woke, majestically, looking radiant and womanly. She assured me nothing had taken part between us, as we were both scuffed the previous evening, due to the quantity and quality of wines. We lay there naked for a short while chatting away whilst her house maid prepared breakfast. I explained to K9 that my days of wondering were almost to an end, due to Nadine giving birth and eventually she will have returned to her normal physique. K9 assured me this was fine as she was engaged to become engaged to a financial advisor, whom worked in the city. As friends we laid together for a while, enjoying the morning glory. Just before breakfast was served, K9 politely and with grace, used her ample breast to arouse me before using he beautiful lushes' lips and a single finger internally placed to relief me of my gentleman's pressure, before heading downstairs for breakfast.

  With the exception of her wedding, I believe it was the last time I saw K9, her wedding day was a pleasant event, she looked radiant in her tight-fitting white dress. We made love once more straight after the ceremony for old times' sake. She now has three children and by all accounts should not use the name K9 anymore having allowed all three children to suckle from her once magnificent breasts.

Afghanistan

Within a matter of months, the British had won the war in Iraq, the newly terrible dictator Saddam Hussein was captured and executed. A new government was selected by the Allies for the people of Iraq. There streets would be safe and well, history would show that the British improved the lives of all the people in Iraq. Luckily al oil contracts were signed prior to the war, to ensure no squabbling would take place.

I was called into the office early one morning to speak with the Chief of Defence staff, he wanted to personally thank me for my efforts leading the troops, he gave me the exciting news that as a direct result of my leadership I had been nominated for a Knight Commander of the Most Excellent Order of the British Empire (KBE). A couple of chaps were awarded the

Commander of the Most Excellent Order of the British Empire (CBE) but it was pot luck the award you were presented and if your old school chum was in the civil service. Luckily for me 'Gangrene' Saunders played in the second XV at St Pauls and later became a member of the Oscaman Club, therefore a KBE was awarded.

I was also informed that I would be unfortunately returning to frontline duties. I was to return to the 2nd Battalion South Yorkshire and Derbyshire Fusiliers; I was not due to return to a frontline unit however due to a mix up with a lap dancer and rent boy one of the chaps had to resign his commission. There is nothing wrong with homosexuality, plenty of that stuff went off at Thomas Aquinas College, mainly amongst the arty types and media students, but there is something ashamedly wrong with it if you are married to the Brigadiers favourite daughter. As a result, there was a vacancy and myself and the Brigadier shared a love of Rugby, even though he was Oxford, so I was to be promoted to Lieutenant Colonel and shipped off back to the provinces.

  Nadine was happy at the prospect of the forthcoming investiture for myself, she palmed the children off with the Nannies and shopped for a new outfit. Her liposuction and health care plan had restored her back to former glories and she was looking and feeling delectable. We were a happy young family. Her vagina reconstruction had left her rather snug fitting and much to my liking. The nannies we had recruited for Elizabeth and Monty were excellent young girls, personally and kindly selected by Helen. I discussed with Nadine our picture-perfect family, and explained how waiting in a hospital whilst your wife, lays around on a bed is not becoming a knight of the realm and as such I decided I would have a vasectomy. This would ensure no more accidents with Nadine or any subsequent mistresses, should one be required. I calmly came to the decision, after I worked out the costs and relevant health implication of Nadine removing her entire womb. For one thing if she had a hysterectomy, that would be another restructuring of her lady garden and one assumes a lady can only take so much machinery on her vagina and I would be without my matrimonial rights for several months. Decision made Bulldog would be a Jaffa, ha, but the little swimmers had done well and had a good innings.

Within weeks I had found a suitable surgeon and my tubes had been firmly tied. Painful yes but to be fair the nurse did an exquisite job with the razor, even making the old fella look somewhat bigger.

I returned to my original Regiment, granted with a bit of a limp, some of the men assumes I rode a horse to work, judging by their comments, bless them I do enjoy having the banters. Back at the battalion, I once again wore the khaki beret with Rose cap badge and striking yellow plume. I limped onto the parade square a took my place in front of the men. Some of the old faces were still there, the Company Sergeant Major had been promoted to Warrant Officer Class One, Regimental Sergeant Major. He had grown in stature and now was the proud owner of a moustache busy and firm. Making him look like a gentleman, and a warrior. The new Regimental Sergeant Major (RSM) stood in front of the men, and formally introduced me to the regiment, he then read out a list of names of men that had received awards during the Iraq war.

- Warrant Officer Class One Regimental Sergeant Major Brown to be awarded MBE
- Warrant Officer Class Two Company Sergeant Major Doyle to be awarded MBE
- Corporal Hays awarded Military Cross
- Sergeant Taylor Mentioned in Despatches
- Lieutenant Turner Mentioned in Dispatches

    Cheers and a swift and confident applause went around the parade square with each name read out, then the RSM announced

- Lieutenant Colonel Winston Thatcher DSO, QGM to be awarded KBE

    There was stunned silence, the men, obviously in shock and possibly in utter respect stood silently until the RSM bellowed '*clap you bastards*' a muted applause went around, then men silent, dazed by my great news. I had missed those men, and by their respect I am sure they missed me greatly.

It was a joy to be back with the men, they left that parade square all gossiping regarding my return, before off they went to clean their boots, ready for the inspection the next day. I called the physical training team in and spoke with them regarding the state of the regiments first XV. It was agreed by myself that all rugby union player would be excused from boot cleaning duties and they should concentrate on their playing. The Physical Training Team, enjoyed the extra work, getting the rugby team ready. I believe you can tell a lot about a regiment by its first XV.

I got the more senior officers together and we arranged a structure to management, I would have overall final say, after the majors had drawn up a plan, discussed it and then present me their findings. It seemed like a good idea and one that takes away all that unnecessary red tape. My military life was a happy life.

  Then tragedy strook, one ordinary morning, as I arrived at work, a communique arrived, the battalion was yet again to be deployed. This time Afghanistan was calling, after years of supporting the locals fight the Russians, we decided that enough was enough and the Afghans had now become terrorist. As such we would go over to their country and base ourselves near the poppy fields to protect the country and its innocent people, from the face of evil. This was going to be my final push as a fighting soldier, so I summand my senior staff. I explained that we would once again travel to distant shores and fight our enemies. I had the Regimental Sergeant Major parade the men. I knew the speech I was to give would be important to them. For the first time I didn't pen a speech I decided to speak from the heart.

"*Gentlemen, today news has arrived at the Battalion that we the 2nd Battalion South Yorkshire and Derbyshire Fusiliers are to be once again sent to a foreign land to fight a foreign foe. We will stand tall and stand proud, we will meet the challenges head on, and hopefully most of you will be good enough to come back. So tonight, after you have cleaned and polished your kit say goodbye to your loved ones, if you are married make love to your wives and leave them with a smile and a pleasant taste in their mouths. If you are single feel free to phone your families and say goodbye. Explain to them that we the South Yorkshire and Derbyshire Fusiliers will travel to a faraway land, and with pride and British grit destroy the evil that is terrorism, for our loved ones, our American cousins and of course the Queen. We will surround the poppy fields and ensure vital minerals needed by the west are left intact. Our enemies will regret the day, they flew a* *plane into a tower in America, and left their flame proof their passports, identifying them and the country they were raised. Now revenge will strike, firm and it will strike hard."*

I could feel their sense of sadness as I walked away, the deafening silence said it all. I returned to my office and watched from the windows as my men, slowly walked back to their accommodation block to polish their boots and iron their uniforms, some for the last time.

As a mark of respect, I had copies of my speech presented to the Sergeants Mess and Junior Ranks Mess. I knew my words were important to them

I went home that evening and explained to Nadine that the Battalion was to leave with immediate readiness. She looked a little taken aback, she rather beautifully let one single tear run down her beautiful face. She looked up at me, I could tell she was hurting and I could see she wanted to speak, her beautiful lips quivering. I gently placed my hand on her shoulder and looked into her beautiful striking blue eyes and I gently smiled. I then lovingly said to her in a romantic tone, "so off to the bedroom you pop, put on some stockings and a thong and let's get this over with." Before gently slapping her tight firm backside. That night for the first time ever I made love to my wife, gently, and with loving strokes, looking into her beautiful eyes, savouring every second with her. It was also the first time I finished on her face!

The next morning, I waved goodbye to Monty and Elizabeth, I kissed my beautiful wife, now she had showered and washed her face. I slapped her on her backside and stepped out of the house, ready once again for war.

At the Battalion the men were ready to go, we set off for Royal Air Force Station Brize Norton and another chapter in the Regimental history pages.

We arrived in Afghanistan and my first thought was, what a complete shit hole, I couldn't see one good thing about the place, the camp was a dump. We had to share with the Americans and some Canadians it was dusty and dirty and not good at all. The Officers Mess was well below par, my accommodation was substandard, the entire place was bloody horrible. I spent most of my first night writing to Political and military leaders in the United Kingdom regarding my unhappiness. The men were left alone to unpack before they settled in and within a day of arriving our work had started.

The men were either out patrolling or cleaning uniforms as the desert winds and dirt made them look unprofessional. I had my leadership team keep me up to date with all the goings on.

Day twenty-nine arrived, it was a lovely day, the sun was shining, I had earlier received a lovely letter form Nadine and a rather splendid photograph of the children. Helen and Sara also wrote me a lovely message and sent a picture of both women stood in just their stockings, I assumed it was meant for Racheal as the message on the back of the photo was addressed to her, I assume they accidently forwarded it on to me. However, it took pride of place in my bed space and help me with my night time relaxation.

As I was in a good mood, I went to see the Regimental Sergeant Major, I explained to him that I would pop out with the men on a patrol. Bless him, the man loved and respected me so much he begged me not to come. How he was extremely apprehensive about my safety and that really touched me. However, I was having none of it and insisted on patrolling with my men.

At 10:00 hours we jumped into our vehicles and set off on patrol, to be honest the first half an hour was uneventful. So, to liven things up I talked to our driver one of the Lance Corporals and we decided we would pull over at the side of the road and have a platoon photograph for perpetuity.

The Regimental Sergeant Major again worried for my safety tried to prevent this but I insisted and informed him the men would take that picture with them to their graves with pride. As the vehicle pulled over to the side of the road, the driver foolishly hit an Improvised Explosive Device and all hell broke loose.

I remember being catapulted into the air and landing at the side of the vehicle, in a form of agony I had never witnessed before. It took the medic some time to come to my assistance, for which I had him charged and demoted, the Medical Corps only have one job and if they take their time treating lower ranks first, well to be fair what is the point of them.

A helicopter arrived and took myself a Lance Corporal and a Sergeant back to base for emergency medical treatment. I myself broke a bone in my foot and badly sprained my ankle with landing in an awkward position. Lance Corporal Jones lost his right leg and Sergeant Hope lost his right arm and his right leg, due to taking the brunt of the explosion months later he was reduced to the rank of Corporal after he failed to shake my hand at the Regimental home coming. I fully accept he had injuries and his right arm was somewhere in Afghanistan but standards must always be upheld.

The medical experts ignoring my sprained ankle had tried to save the limbs of the men however it wasn't to be.

As a senior officer the war was over for me and I was to be sent back to Britain for treatment. Many people believe when you leave the war zone the suffering ends, but what they fail to understand is the military hospital was in bloody Birmingham. It was jumping out of the frying pan into the bloody fire.

I spent a few weeks in the hospital but I have to be honest, I found the National Health Service food to be unacceptable and therefore I was allowed back to my wife and family to recover from my horrific injuries. Despite being in a private room, I could still hear the lower ranks, speaking, moaning and complaining, it really did spoil my stay in hospital

I made an almost full recovery, granted my Rugby days are over, but all the best things must sadly come to an end. Some of the chaps in Whitehall were distressed with my news, and without a moment of hesitation I posted back to Whitehall and an office job, life on the front line was no good for a Lieutenant Colonel with a dicky ankle.

I did make it back to the battalion to see the men arrive back from the war and for the medal presentation. Having served over twenty-eight days I was rightfully presented my medal first. As I stood there resting on my walking stick, I looked at my men, all proud and presentable. The injured soldiers were there, Lance Corporal 'Leggy' Jones and Corporal Hope. I had both men Mentioned in Dispatches. It was the least I could do and the thought of having such an honour may take the edge off losing a limb, or two in Sergeant Hopes case.

I realised my time within a fighting unit sadly was coming to an end. I would now have to lead my men from the heart of Government, sat in my office in Whitehall. Had I been an emotional man I may have spared a tear or two. But crying isn't for a gentleman.

I later spoke with Nadine and explained my decision to leave the military and how I would now be office based until my retirement. She accepted my decision and gently masturbated me as I reeled off my plans for the future.

Future

My life has been made complete. I was happy and I was finally awarded for my hard work. Sat there in Whitehall was this strapping Lieutenant Colonel Sir Winston 'Bulldog' Thatcher KBE DSO OGM. Who would have thought for one minute when I entered this world the child of a multi-millionaire, Army officer? The nephew to three military officers, the grandchild to two military officers, that I would be able to become a senior officer within the British Army. The odds must be outrageously high. However, here I was a senior officer, proud father of two lovely children, a married man to a woman I truly love a beautiful, caring, loving woman, whom happens to have a spankingly good arse, and due to advances in surgery she has a tight vagina. My wife has regained her pre-birth figure and my children blessed to carry on the family name, well one of them will, the girl will probably marry.

As I now look forward, I can see years of happiness at the house, children growing up, Nadine riding me into the sunset. How I became so fortunate I do not honestly know, probably hard work and determination.

I have had some good years and I have had some good times; I have good friends. Pinkie is still around and still friends with Jean-Paul and Ja'quan, they all share a flat in Notting Hill Ja'quan works high up in the BBC, we often meet for lunch occasionally, bloody good chap he is. Jean – Paul works for Channel Four he is a lovely chap, good company at dinner parties, he has a life partner called Hugh, yes that's right the gays can now marry, to be honest, wasn't sure at first but Jean-Paul and Hugh make a lovely couple and they host a stunning BBQ, amazing what the gays can do with a spit roast.

  Pinkie still works for independent television, shame he never married, but he is always happy and surrounded by pretty people so he is happy, I love that man dearly.

  Sawdust is happily married to a lady banker from the city, roughish looking type but minted. He had a candid affair with her and during one coke fuelled evening they fell in love, divorced their partners and married each other.

  Sara and Helen are still together, both ladies have received plastic surgery and now neither of them shows any sign of surprise, but they are very happy, they adopted a child from the far east and have a stunning family.

  Growler married a lady from Cornwall, she is a lovely lady, who just happens to look like a fisherman.

My children are happy and will soon be ready for boarding school. Myself and Nadine will no doubt travel and enjoy the later years. I will be sad to say goodbye to the military and I will miss slipping into the uniform. But life moves on and as I believe Churchill once said 'forward is in front of us.'

So tonight, I will sip one more glass of Port, smoke my cigar, and contemplate my finer years as a leading military figure.

I have learnt a lot on my journey, for example, the working classes that join the military are good chaps. A gentleman should never drink in a public house with a flat roof. Debutants come and go, so don't worry if you lose one, another will pop along soon enough.

Am I happy you ask, yes I am, like all men I have struggled and I have laughed, I have loved and I have been loved, tonight I will go home my final day as a soldier, I will hug my beautiful wife and contemplate my life so far, before Nadine and I celebrate my career by having a few glasses of wine and indulging in a night of rough love making followed by a golden shower.

Acknowledgements

So, who does Winston want to acknowledge? To be fair no one, I did this my bloody self, I didn't get a hand out from the welfare state, or any other such vile thing. I went to a good boarding school fine university all paid for by father. I gained a commission based on grades, again paid for by father. I was accepted into the military because of my father and uncles. I didn't get handouts I did this all on my bloody own.

I of course would like to acknowledge Nadine, a beautiful lady with firm thighs a tight set of buttocks and a heart of gold. She gave me two beautiful children, and had her vagina tightened after each birth, so old bulldog could still feel the sensation of warm surroundings as he pleasured his wife. Nadine has given me much over the years, orgasms, children, friendship and what I like to call a home. A place a man can go, slip into a comfortable dressing robe, light a fine Cuban, and receive oral all in his sitting room.

Sir Guy Cheshire, KBE, AFC, RAF (ret'd) thank you for writing my words and for being a bloody good chap.

The ladies I have pleasured over the years, those girls have given me minutes of pleasure and memories I will take with me to the large parade square in the sky. From lovely, delicate Sarah and her cute smile, Tamara and her flexible approach to K9 and her ample bosoms, I have enjoyed my love making almost as much as the ladies did.

My dear, dear friends, friends for their support, their laughter and their warmth they have always shown, many a time I have laughed at the poor and the vulnerable with my friends. times I remember fondly.

The virgins I have met, thanks for nothing.

To you the reader, thank you for opening your heart, your wallet and your time to allow me to tell you a story of heroics and horrors, warmth and passion. I know I have inspired each and every one of you to be a better person and finer friend. I know that after reading this book you will be full of pride and you will probably service your wife/girlfriend in a more vigorous manner. Tell her from me, 'you're welcome.'

© MMXX **Robert E Harris**

This book and its content are copyright of Robert E Harris - © Robert Harris 2021 All rights reserved. Any redistribution or reproduction of part or all of the contents in any form is prohibited

Printed in Great Britain
by Amazon